Bedlam's
PLAYGROUND

Edited by: ProofsbyPolly

Paperback ISBN: 978-1-990675-58-4

CONTENT WARNING

THIS NOVELLA CONTAINS THE FOLLOWING:
BLOOD
MURDER
GHOST RAPE
SEXUAL DEGRADATION
EXPLICIT SEX SCENES
BROTHER ON BROTHER
POSSESSION

IF YOU ARE SENSITIVE TO ANY OF THE
ABOVE CONTENT, PLEASE DO NOT
CONTINUE.

READER'S DISCRETION IS ADVISED

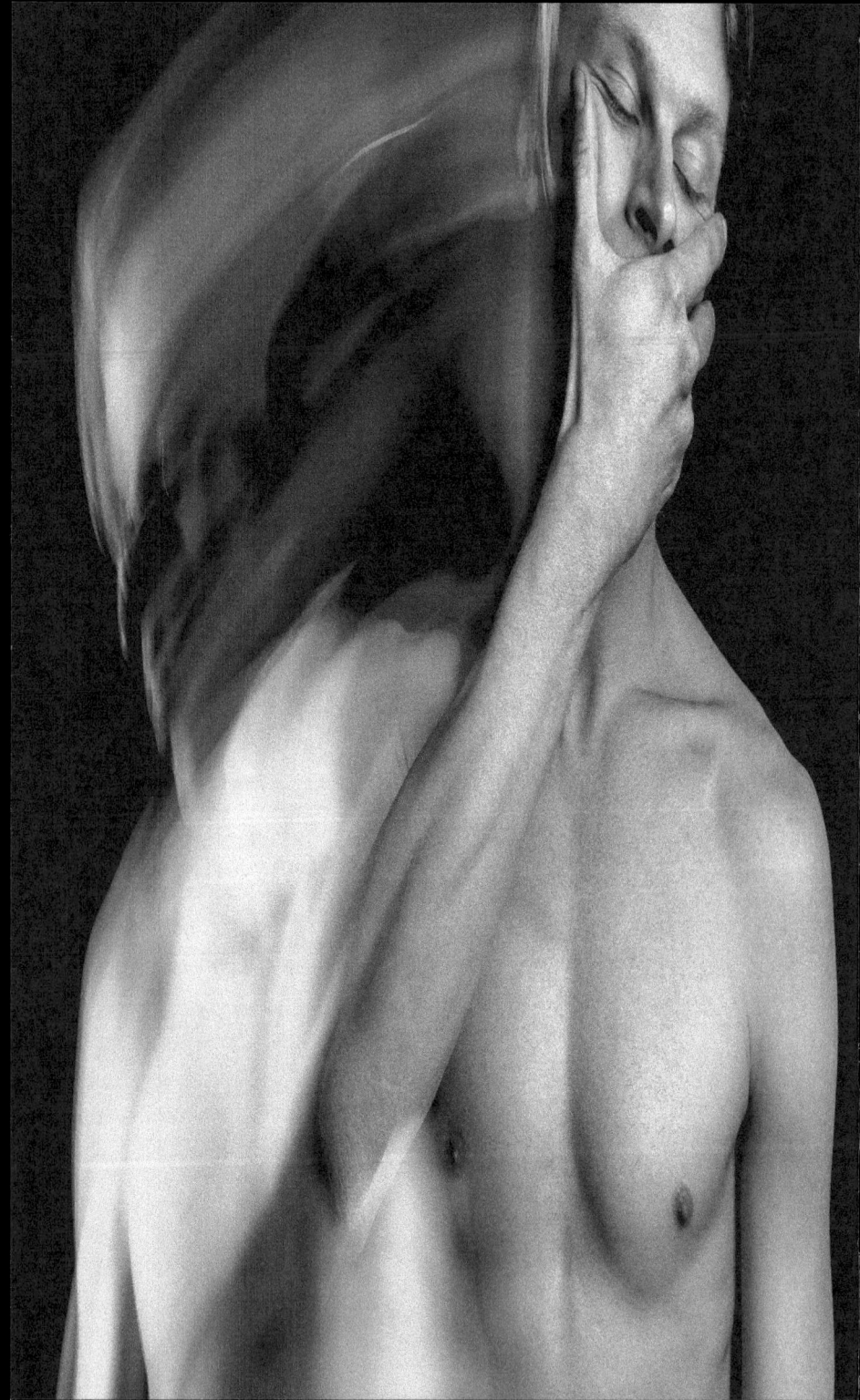

PROLOGUE
<u>Bellgrove Park - Asylum for the mentally insane 1953</u>

The torch cracks as sparks fly across the hall, landing on the linoleum tile and melting into the floor. The smell of melted iron and gas fills the narrow corridor, but breathing the fumes is safer than dealing with the monster who resides on the other side of the industrial door.

"This is inhumane," Charlie mutters as he watches Marvin work the torch. No matter what his morals are, he's still watching as we seal the beast inside the room, having come to terms with our decision. He knows morals have no effect on the Devil.

"He's killed three orderlies today, Charlie!" Marvin huffs as he wipes the sweat from his brow using his forearm as the torch's flame continues its path along the door.

"We could've called the cops—"

"You know as well as I do, Harold, no cop will step a foot into Bellgrove Park," Marvin cuts me off as he turns off the torch.

The three of us stare transfixed at the door in front of us and the silence that greets us. He's not begging for his life, there are no sounds slipping through the steel door. It almost feels like the room is empty. Not that he spoke much to begin with. The demon of a man trapped inside his cell was never known to be eloquent, preferring actions over his voice.

"He's in there, right?" Charlie whispers, voicing my thoughts.

"He's been jacketed and strapped to the bed," Marvin confirms. "He's not getting out … ever."

"We should've shot him dead," I snarl, anger flooding me as we stare at the gleaming metal door.

"Then he'd never suffer the way he deserves to," Marvin says, giving me a sinister smile. "Let him know true suffering."

That's when I finally take in the scene around me. Our bloodied clothing, the blood splattered on the walls, and the two bodies lying broken on the floor. On the first floor above our heads, the third is still sitting at the front desk, with her head missing.

"What do we do with them?" I choke on the words as the brutality hits me full force.

"We bury them, and then we carry on with life here at Bellgrove. The other patients will live the rest of their days never knowing what's sealed beneath their feet," Marvin states as he pulls off his gloves. "First, we make sure no one else will ever want to open this door."

Marvin grabs a can of red spray paint from his tool kit and shakes it, the noise deafening in the otherwise silent corridor.

Then he begins to spray the door.

No evil will speak.

No evil will see.

No evil will hear.

We seal the door and we seal our fear.

This man is a monster who should have never been here.

We seal this door, we seal this man.

The Devil cannot play on this land.

The words ring loud in my head as Charlie whispers each line while they're being sprayed, and it feels like an incantation.

The paint runs off the edge of each letter, mimicking the blood as it drips down the walls. Conroy Davies entered Bellgrove Park

Bedlam's Playground

as criminally insane, and he'll stay sealed inside these walls for all eternity, never seeing the light of day again.

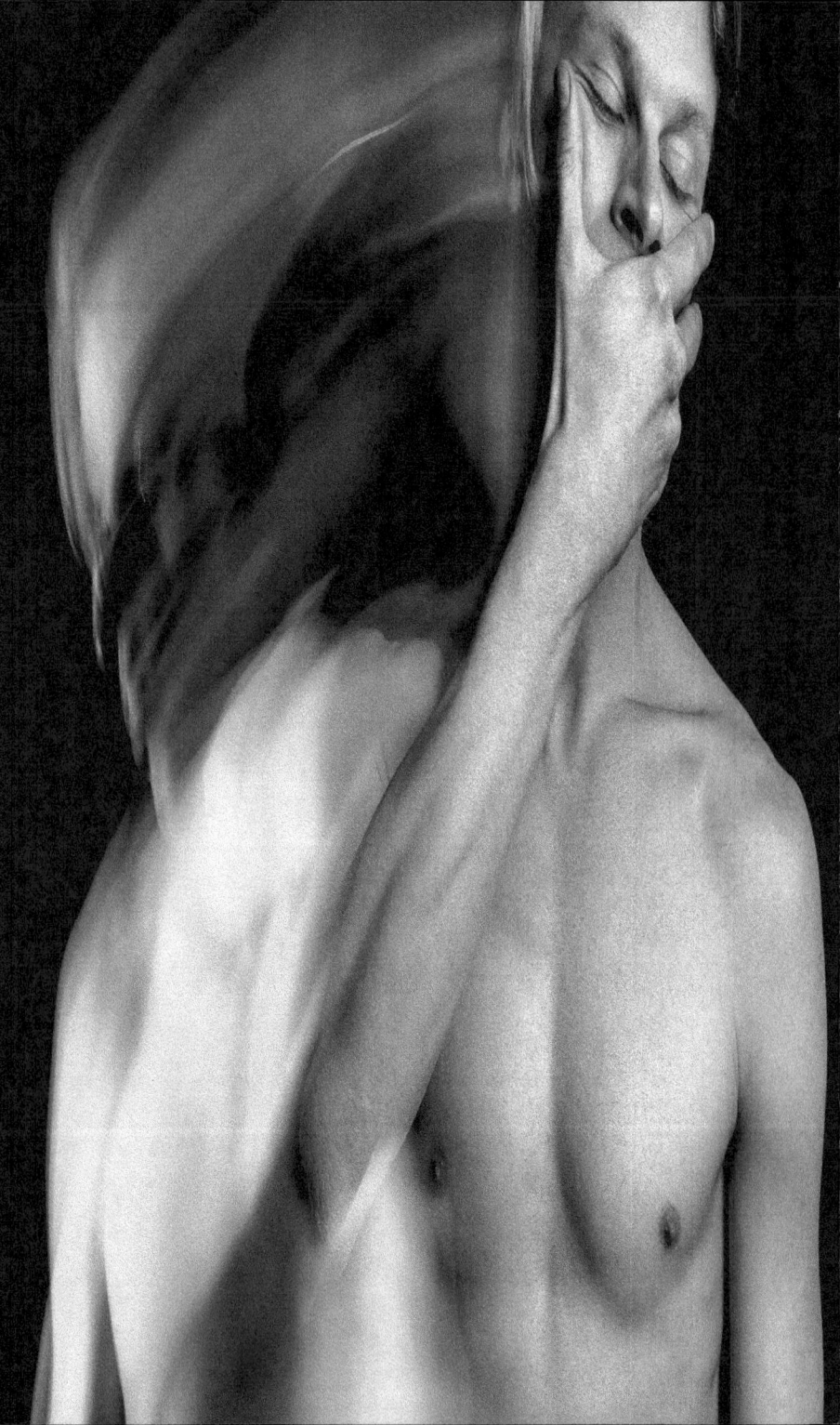

ONE

Connor

<u>**Present Day**</u>

The earth will always reclaim the land that humans destroy.

The thought breezes through my mind as I stare at what once was a beautiful, flowing fountain now covered in vines and disgusting sludge collected at the bottom. The building looming behind it doesn't look much better. The three-story monster whose stones hold secrets we want to find has busted-out windows and trees growing from inside.

"Connor! Quit dicking around and help us unload, dude!" I hear Nick snap and look over to where our two vans are parked in the circular drive in front of the building. All of the doors are open and our equipment is to the point of falling out which is a crying shame considering how much money we've invested in it. "We have tonight only, and I don't want to waste any more time with setup. We need to be streaming soon because we promised the fans an inside look at our setup process," Nick orders again. The fucking prick thinks he's the owner of our crew, but really, he just has a good brain that he doesn't always use. I can always rely on Nick to push a pull door and look for his phone as he is talking on it.

I trot over and grab a heavy box from Mary, the only woman in this operation and the single, most distracting thing for me in this crew.

"Thanks. I thought I was about to give myself a hernia tugging that heavy piece of shit," she says, rubbing her back and stretching it out by pushing her chest forward. I forget momentarily what the fuck I'm supposed to be doing as I watch her barely-there tits push out against the tank top she's wearing. She's gorgeous and doesn't even realize it. She also has the three of us wrapped around her pinky finger.

So many times I've dreamed about having this woman, but never had the courage to even slightly flirt with her because I poured myself into books instead of girls growing up and I never practiced the approach as Nick likes to say. My dick better not pop a stiffy right now cause the last time that happened I spent the entire investigation holding a camera in front of me to hide it.

"No problem," I reply like a dumbass as she straightens. She gives me a coy smile, and it's on the tip of my tongue to say something, anything, to compliment her. Before I even get a chance to, a bug straight from the pits of Hell flies in my mouth, causing me to start coughing and gagging while I damn near drop the box to get the fucking insect dislodged. Having made myself look like an idiot in front of her once again, I blush hard and turn my back to her so she doesn't see the strain on my face from holding in another cough and the tears pricking my eyes. I beat my chest a couple of times and get ahold of myself before looking back at her one more time to see her attention isn't even on my near-death experience, but on the building, and send up a silent thank you to whatever is listening.

I turn and walk away from her quickly, placing the heavy box of drop cords on the steps where the rest of the boxes and bags are being unloaded. Most of the equipment is zip tied and tagged out to stay as organized as possible, so I grab my knife out of my pocket to start clipping and unrolling some cords out.

An uneasy feeling of being watched comes over me, and I freeze. It's not uncommon for this type of feeling to hit when we investigate haunted locations for a living, but something about this place feels more sinister than any location we've been to before.

I glance up at the window on the second floor where I feel eyes on me and nothing but a quick shadow crossing in front of it greets me. A quick moment of uncertainty hits me, and I hear a whisper tickle my brain that this could very well become my tomb if I enter this building. I've never chickened out before and I'm not about to start now, but this feeling like I could never leave this place hits me strongly, and I almost debate saying something to the others.

"Hey, guys! Check this out! That box of old records the owner gave us has a map of the building, reports from former workers, and one hell of a wicked story about a cellblock that was sealed shut with a patient still inside!" James says, startling me from my musings and drawing my attention back to the crew.

"Seriously, you nerd. We need to get everything unloaded before you jizz yourself with old records. Boxes first, history porn later," Nick orders, grabbing another box out of the van that holds our personal camcorders and dropping them at his feet.

"Hey! Those are fragile!" I gripe, running over and checking the precious electrical little ones for damage. As I said, this shit is expensive and top-of-the-line.

"Great. One of you has a boner for history and the other for electronics. I'm in nerd hell," Nick mutters as he grabs another box.

Mary

I leave them to argue amongst themselves and head up to the large front door. There's a thick industrial chain wrapped around the metal door handles, and the lock sealing it shut had long rusted away.

My fingers skim the dark orange surface as thick flakes slowly float to the ground at my feet. The hairs on the back of my neck begin to rise as I sense something looming beyond these doors. It's not trepidation, although I should be feeling that. Instead, it's an urgency to get through the chain and step into the building.

Something is calling to me.

"Did you know this was a secret facility?" James' deep voice slips over my heated skin, nearly pulling forth a groan from my mouth. These guys are supposed to be my best friends and teammates, and they are, but I've been denying my true feelings for them for years. This past year has proven they'll never fade, and our relationship will only grow stronger the longer we stay together.

"I read something like that." I nod, the husky inflection in my voice surprising me. My eyes flick to James, wondering if he's feeling the shift between us.

He steps closer to me, his cologne dousing me in a cloud

11

of need, and I clench my thighs to stave it off. This is not the time or place.

"Bellgrove Park was home to the most criminally insane on one side of the facility, and then a state-run home for children and teens suffering from mild to severe afflictions on the other."

"Children too?" I look over my shoulder at him, meeting his amber irises with shock.

"Yeah." He nods, his full mouth tipping downward. "Any child or teen showing signs of desire for the same sex were shipped off here for special electroshock therapy."

"Oh, no." I cover my mouth with my hands as despair rolls through me.

I'm not a stranger to abuse, especially at the hands of people who are meant to take care of you. Nothing much shocks me these days, and I repeat that every time we hit up a new place, only to be shocked at the vile past it holds.

"Criminals whose mental states prevented them from standing trial came here. Children born with deformities and developmental issues were shipped off to live their lives here. And then there are the few who were held in the basement, a ward for the dangerous."

"Conroy Davies," I whisper, my eyes returning to the rusted lock.

"Yeah," James continues behind me. His words begin to sound rushed as he feels the excitement of this abandoned building. He always was attracted to these places, more so than the rest of us. My guess is they invoke his love of solving mysteries. "He went on a rampage in Pensacola, hitting up all the Girl Guide's camps, raping and then murdering young girls. He admitted to a judge that young girls brought out urges he couldn't suppress. He was sent here."

"With children." The words are spit out from between my teeth. The complete disregard for the children who were here hits me full in the chest.

"Mentally deranged and physically deformed children," James reiterates, voicing my thoughts. "Practically nobodies."

The surface of my skin erupts with goose bumps as my eyes

water, the chain in front of me distorting with my tears.

"The story goes something like this: He was sent here on a Tuesday, and by Thursday, he had already made his way over to the children's side, having killed two orderlies to escape the basement."

My body shudders with distress, my own trauma threatening to rise along with the bile coursing up my throat.

"The front clerk—a middle-aged woman—heard the alarms, alerting the facility to a breakout. She picked up the phone to call the police, only to have her head chopped off, the phone still gripped in her palm."

James is a fantastic storyteller, his deep, gravelly tone keeps us listeners intrigued. This is why we have him as the one in front of the camera when it comes time to tell the history of the location.

It doesn't hurt that he embellishes some points too. I highly doubt he knows for sure whether the phone was still in her palm, but it causes another shudder to rip through me anyway.

"He'd only defiled one young girl by the time he was caught," James intones. "They shot him with a tranq, then hauled him back down to the basement. They wrapped him in a straitjacket and strapped him to the bed." He steps in closer to my back, his warm breath hitting my moisture-coated skin. The story is ominous, much like the energy seeping out from behind the door. I can feel it and can't seem to pull my eyes away from the wooden surface. "Then they sealed the door."

"He's still in there?" My eyes widen on him with shock. Surely, that can't be the case.

"So they say." He steps around me, his voice losing its reverence, storytime being over.

James' wide body steps in front of me, his shoulders rippling as he lifts the bolt cutters and snaps the lock off the chain. My eyes stay trained on the bulging veins of his arms, and I swallow down yet another bout of lust. I've always held an appreciation for James' beauty, but it's growing into something beyond simple admiration.

This is getting out of hand.

The heavy chains slip from the handles, landing on the ground in a chorus of *clinks* and *clanks*. James faces me then, grabbing a wayward, brunette curl before it flies in front of my face and tucks it behind my ear, sending arcs of electricity along my skin.

"Are you ready, Mary?"

Then the very same long, tattooed fingers wrap around the handle, giving it a yank. Nothing happens.

"What the fuck?" he snaps, his eyes settling on me with bewilderment.

"Maaaaary... Are you quite contrary?"

"Did you hear that?" I step forward, dismissing James' look of confusion. "There's someone in there."

"Mary," he growls out, "save the theatrics for when we're actually inside the place."

I ignore him as I run my fingers along the heavy, oak door. It feels cold, too cold, making the tips of my fingers frigid as my hand replaces his on the handle.

"It's locked," James calls out to the guys. "We need the pick kit."

With a firm grip, I pull on the handle, and the door opens smoothly, the rusted hinges not making a sound.

"What the fuck?" James repeats, his eyes willing me to believe him. "That was locked."

I do believe him. I bet it was locked, but whoever called out to me, wants me to come inside.

The first thing I feel is the cool breeze that hits my face, carrying a scent of disinfectant and moisture. It doesn't smell like the place has been boarded up for the last nearly seventy years. It's dark inside, but some light filters through the cracks in the boards on the windows, highlighting the checkered, mint green and white linoleum floor that has about an inch of dust on it. Looking up, I note with surprise a few light fixtures that have fallen from the ceiling, hanging precariously from the wires.

"This is the creepiest shit yet," Nick breathes out from the step behind me, sounding too excited. Not much phases him or sours his mood. Such a contrast to his big brother, James.

14

I step up to the threshold as James' hand grips my bicep, pulling me back outside and beside him.

"Wait until we have a livestream going," he advises, my eyes still peering into the dark, reception area.

I can see a desk in the center of the room, the mahogany-stained surface muted by the dull gray color of dust. The walls were a mint green to match the floor, but mostly it's yellowed with mold and rot. The plaster is falling off in large chunks as the wide cracks creep along the walls like spiderwebs.

And then there are the actual spider webs. The dust-coated strands look thick and ominous as they hang from every corner like gray drapery. Only the thought of what lurks beneath them has a shiver skating down my spine.

"Going live in … three … two … one …" Nick hands James the phone just as the flash turns on, illuminating the specks of dust in the air.

"Hey, Phantom Lovers," James' deep, husky voice echoes throughout the room as he steps inside. "We're here at Bellgrove Park, the retreat where you can send your problematic children, and claim they're at summer camp … indefinitely."

James

"Here is the receptionist's desk." I point the phone toward the large, looming desk.

The heavy coat of dust covers any evidence of a murder, but I'm hoping once we dig deeper and clear it off, there will be at least some darkened with aged bloodstains the caretakers couldn't clean out completely.

"Here sat Conroy Davies' last victim as she frantically tried to call the police on the rotary dial." I let the camera scan along the top of the desk, slowly bringing into focus the ancient, mint green phone, the cord to the receiver cut, and the receiver itself missing. "Her head was chopped off with the ax he took from the fire station encased in glass. One chop, her scream cut short, and the dial tone sounding from the speaker still clutched in her hand."

My brother, Nick, and our best friend, Connor, begin setting up the filming station in the center of the reception area. After we power up the gas generators, the lights go up, the laptops power on, ready to view the livestream, and our detection equipment is opened, ready to be taken into the scarier parts of the place. But for the single night that we're here, we'll sleep closest to the entrance.

We've stayed in some seriously haunted houses, but nothing has driven us out before our night is up. We have yet to see anything supernatural beyond the fluctuations in our EMF meters, and the movements showing up on our infrareds. The best is when we set up the perimeter laser grids, and laugh when Mary freaks out over the distortions.

My eyes find the girl who's somehow wormed her way inside me and has yet to let me go. At first, I chalked up my new feelings for her to the fact that she grew boobs. Then it was because she was the only girl we hung out with for lengthy periods of time. But now, I know the girl with the unruly mane of brunette hair, big, blue eyes, and sandy-colored skin that always looks tanned is more than a passing crush. I've been trying to work up the courage to ask her out for so long, only to be crushed when she shows one of the other two a little more attention.

Then the cycle starts all over again.

"Nick and Connor are setting up the equipment now," I tell the people who are starting to file onto the live. "Nick will be setting up the laser grid while Connor gets the EMF meters and infrareds up."

I clip the phone onto the stand Connor has already set up, and my eyes wander again until they find Mary standing in front of a large, winding staircase, her head angled upward as she looks to the second floor. She has a beauty mark that rests just to the right of her top lip, the brown spot accentuating her appeal and constantly winning my attention. She whines about it looking like a malignant growth, while I think it makes her look like a supermodel.

My boots echo around the room as I head toward her. As per usual, I'm stuck in her gravitational pull, and this is where I'll orbit until she chooses one of us. The guys and I have spoken about it to great lengths because each of them is feeling similar to the way I am. Whoever she picks, the other two will step back without a problem, and support the couple. But we've also spoken about her picking all of us, and how much easier it would be if she did. There would be no jealousy, and we would all take care of her, just like we already do.

As much as the three of us pine for the girl we grew up living next door to, we all know something happened to her when she was younger, and it's changed how she views relationships. She doesn't date, doesn't entertain men who give her longing looks, and she doesn't reciprocate any of our flirting. She's nineteen this year and has never had a boyfriend … or girlfriend.

"What are you looking at?" I stand behind her and take in a deep breath, inhaling the scent of strawberries in her shampooed hair. This is my favorite thing to do, and strawberries have become a favorite of mine.

"Minor Ward," she reads off the sign hanging from one corner, the chain looking ready to snap like it did on the other side. Her hand rises as she points upstairs where the arrow would if it was hung properly. "Adult Ward." Her hand moves to the opposite side of the stairs on the second floor. "And Lockdown." Her finger, adorned with a large, chunky, skull ring, points down into the blackened abyss of the basement. "Finally, Bedlam's Playground." She points ahead toward a set of boarded-off doors at the back of the large mansion. "Why would they call it that?"

Bedlam's Playground was the outdoor section where they would let the children and adults go for sunlight and fresh air. "Sick sense of humor." I shrug. "It was where the patients were let out to frolic."

"They're still here, James." Her voice sounds small as her arms encircle her waist. "Can you feel them?"

My eyes drift along to the second floor. The dark shadows are still, and the only sounds that can be heard are coming from the guys as they set up and speak into the camera. I wait to feel whatever it is she's feeling, but there's nothing. I start to shake my head, only to be interrupted by the sound of Nick dropping a box to the floor, the loud crash reverberating around the cavernous space.

"Save it for the camera, yeah?" My hand grips her shoulder, and I don't miss the way she stiffens, as if the touch is invoking painful memories.

Nick

Switching on the laser grid, I see Mary jump a little as the green rays startle her and I smile to myself. That girl gets scared of a leaf being blown across the floor. She's stuck it out with us for this long. One would think she'd start getting accustomed to this, but that's one thing I really like about her. She barely changes who she is and to me, that's her being perfect. I know her past haunts her, pun intended, and her strength to push herself out of her comfort zone makes me see her beauty as much more than just a face. It's her soul I'm attracted to.

"Hey, can you hand me—" I start to say to Connor when my wrench is slid across the dusty floor toward me.

"You always forget it, dude," Connor replies to my baffled face. The cheeky fucker. I make my last few adjustments, angling the grid to hit all corners of the room before I stand and admire my handy work. It took the will of God for Connor to show me how to step this shit up to cut down on installation time so we could start the investigations sooner. I'm glad he did, so I don't feel so useless in the group. Yeah, I may arrange the locations by sweet-talking the owners, but beyond that, I have nothing more to offer our group.

I glance back over to where my brother is chatting away with Mary, likely pointing shit out to her, and a moment of jealousy hits me. I wish someone looked at me like I was their hero for once. Mary doesn't realize she's even doing it is the icing on the cake. I let the jealousy go because my big brother has never let a moment of our lives pass where he'd ever let me feel like I didn't belong and if he could hear my thoughts right now, he'd kick my ass for them.

An old baseball comes rolling past my foot, and I quickly snatch up my camcorder and point it in the direction it came from. I click it on and snap my fingers to the others, first pointing at the ball rolling, then back in the direction I'm moving. Not going to lie, this shit creeps me out all the time, but I've never felt more alive than when the adrenaline rush of the unknown shows face.

James quickly comes over and grabs the cell phone that's streaming, filling in the fans that we already got activity in which we are going to verify or debunk. I keep my camera pointed at the corner of the great entryway, scanning all around with my eyes, trying to catch a shadow or something to help explain the ball. When I creep in closer, I hear a hissing sound and throw my arm out to stop Connor from moving ahead as he records on his camcorder.

I'm finally certain it's not a snake as I lean in closer, seeing a dark tail zip behind an old couch, I get down on my belly and zoom in, only to find a fucking raccoon and his beady eyes staring back at me. Fucking little trash panda made his home in a damn asylum. What irony.

"Sorry, guys, looks like this one is debunked, but have no fear, we always deliver great footage of activity to you. And from the feel of this place, I'm certain it's crawling with it," James speaks with the fans, and I switch my camera off. Sitting back on my heels, I turn and look back at the baseball. A small, little shadow looms over it and we all catch a child-like giggle before it vanishes.

"Fuck, did you get that?!?" I ask Connor, and he shakes his head, showing me he switched his camera off too.

Fuck this. I stand and brush off my pants, heading over to where the baseball is. If we're dealing with kids, which we more than likely are since there's a minor's ward, Mary will probably be our best bet to bring them out of hiding. She has a gentle and kind spirit that puts the children at ease in her presence.

Once I grab the ball, I head over to her.

"Think you can get some kiddos to play ball with us in the children's ward, sunshine?" I chirp out the nickname I gave her in my head unintentionally and wince hard. She looks me up and down with a face of amusement, then smiles softly.

"Yeah, I think I can manage that one," she replies but looks really uncertain. I want to kiss away her worries and fears, but I know better because the one time I tried to soothe her, she almost kneed me in the balls for it. She can be a spitfire when she wants to and never fails to amaze me with her bravery. It's not like ghosts can harm us beyond some scratches and throwing shit at us.

"As long as Nick doesn't start antagonizing the spirits again, I think we will have a nice and easy investigation," James says, sliding up beside us.

"It was one time! How was I supposed to know a pissed off chef ghost would get mad enough to throw hot grease at us 'cause I called his burgers shit? I mean really, we had it coming investigating a haunted fucking diner, anyway. What ghost lingers around his workplace? A stupid one, that's what," I finish my rant of that fucking joint. It was a joke. Then again, we got great documented activity from there.

"Just don't start any bullshit here. This place has a don't fuck with the dead vibe, and I'm not trying to have anything attach to us and follow us home, if you catch my drift," James clips out, giving me a pointed look.

"Poltergeists are rare, dude. You know this as much as I do. In all the places we've been to, we haven't come across a single one, so what makes this place so different, huh?" I say, stretching my arms wide to get my point across.

"No other place sealed a fucking psychopath in the fucking basement like they've done here. I'm about to head down there and check that out, as a matter of fact, to confirm its existence." James finishes by walking away and grabbing his equipment to take with him. That fucker isn't going to have all the fun.

"Well, guys, as you can see, the brothers are going head-to-head again. We will be signing back on a little bit later once we are set and ready to go. Leave us some comments below on where you'd like to see us go while we're in here. Bye!" Mary says to the phone before clicking out the livestream. I didn't even notice James had passed the phone off to her.

"I think we need to start marking out our locations first for setup. We have plenty of time to hit the basement," Connor chimes in with an uneasy tone.

"Are you scared, my guy?" I laugh in disbelief. Connor has always been a little awkward, but scared? Never.

Maybe I should give some caution to this place, because I'm feeling slightly on edge.

Bedlam's Playground

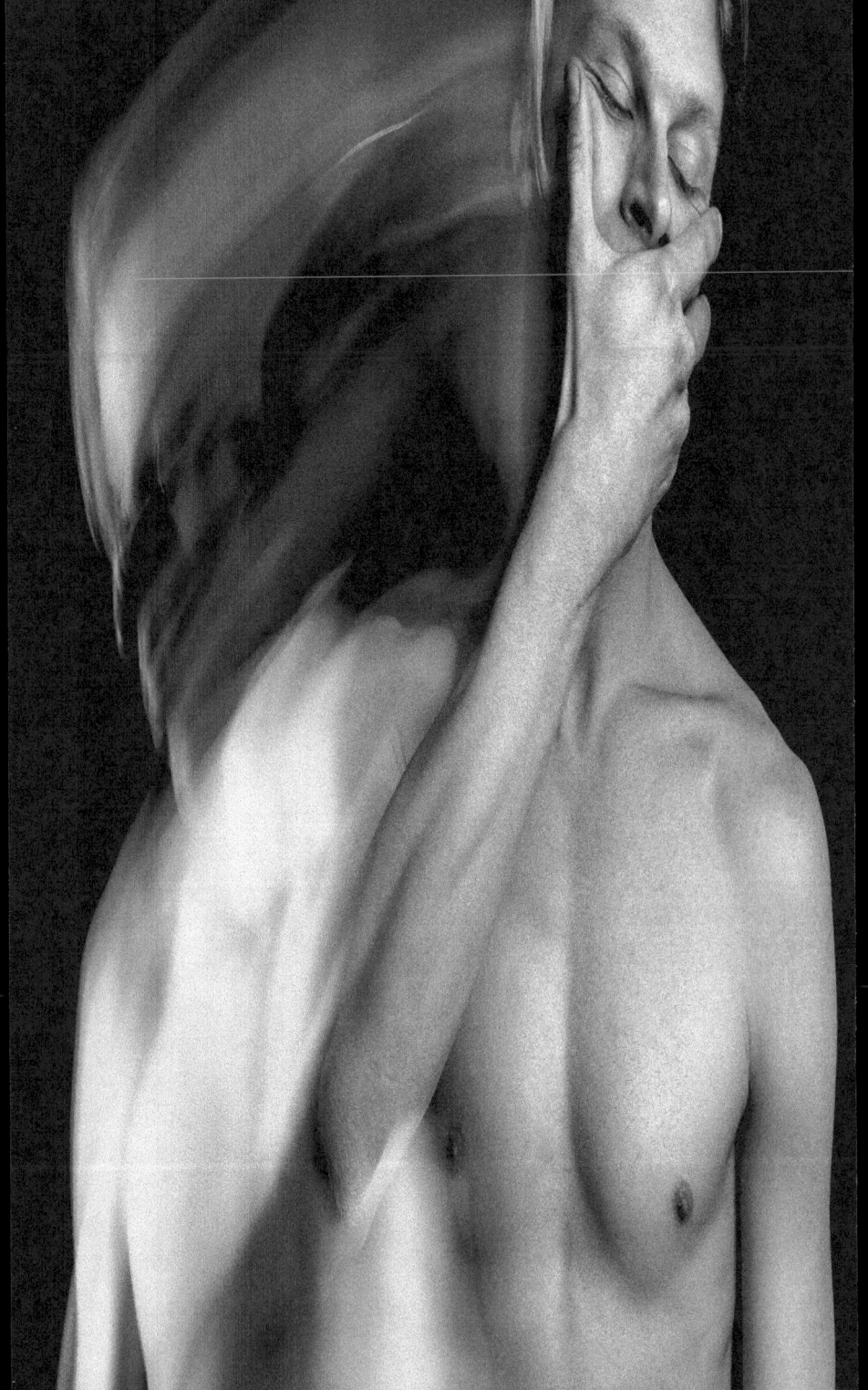

TWO
James

Nicky only taunts me when he's jealous about how close Mary and I are getting. We've had a talk, and even though we all came to a consensus about our feelings, his still gets the better of him.

He's rash, speaks out of pocket, and has the energy of a squirrel on fucking crack. It's also why he's a crowd favorite. None of us are rich. We rely on the PayPal and Venmo donations we receive during the streams, and more times than not, they pile in when Nick is being his crazy self.

My boot steps down onto the first stair to the basement when Connor grips my bicep.

"Dude," he whispers, not wanting Mary or Nick to hear. "I don't feel so good about this place, especially that basement."

"Connor," I turn on him with an exasperated look. "We are here *for* the basement. I need to know if that door exists, and then we need to film it so we can make some flow. Understand?"

"It's not worth it if we're dead," he snaps, his face a mask of annoyance.

"Dead?" My voice is filled with perplexity as I lean in.

He doesn't have a chance to answer me as Mary and Nick stride up to us.

"We're really doing this right now?" Mary asks, her voice shaking as she turns on the handheld EMF meter.

"It's better to get it over with during the day, right?" My hand lands on her shoulder, reassuring her she's safe.

"Down there? It makes no difference between day and night," Connor says, his voice sounding far away in our close proximity. "No light can penetrate these concrete walls."

"The fuck is wrong with you?" Nick twists his head so his face is right in Connor's.

"It's cold," Connor says as he begins to descend the stairs.

"It is cold down there," I say to Mary, my eyes wandering over her tank top and hardened nipples. "Did you want to grab your sweater?"

"I'm fine." Nick waves me off and starts down the stairs after Connor. "Thanks for looking out, bro."

"I'm going to kill him before any ghost gets the chance," I grit out through my teeth.

"He does it for your reactions." Mary chuckles. "You give in every time."

"He should keep his parental issues in check." I grin at her. "We both had shit-for-brains parents, but I think I turned out all right."

Her mouth tips upward, but the smile doesn't reach her blue eyes. Shit, that was insensitive, considering Mary's parents died when she was younger, and she was sent to live with her mother's brother and his wife.

I know the things that happened in that house when she was growing up, but I can't bring myself to hate the situation completely. It brought her right next door to me and Nick. She was a ray of sunshine in our gloomy lives, hence why Nick calls her that. She would brighten our days, even when hers were just as dismal.

The first step she takes down the stairs has her gasping for breath. I can feel it too, the way the air turns cooler, the feel of it heavy with moisture. I link my hand with hers and give it a squeeze. I wouldn't let anything happen to her.

Mary holds the meter out in front of her, the needle moving rapidly back and forth. "We haven't even stepped foot in the basement, and this thing is moving more than it ever has."

24

"Guys!" I call out to my brother and Connor. "We have movement." I motion with my hand for Mary to hand me back my phone and load up the livestream.

I know we said we would check it out first, but this is the shit that loosens the wallets. I pull up our website and log into the blog, preparing to start filming just as Connor and Nick appear in front of us, both of them riveted on the meter.

As soon as I post the link to the site, fifty people jam in within a minute.

"Guys," I point the camera toward the dark basement, putting on a more breathless tone. They love when we sound scared. "We were going to wait until we had a good look around down there before going live again, but look at this meter, and we're only at the top of the stairs."

My idea of charging a premium subscription is becoming more feasible as our phones begin to ping with PayPal and Venmo notifications. Comments flood the screen. People are freaked out, amped up, and even watching in groups at home like some Sunday night drama.

We all fall silent and let the ticking of the meter fill the space, giving the feed a more sinister vibe. Nick is the first one to go back down the stairs, and I keep the camera pointed at his back. Mary grips the meter, the device trembling a little as she, too, heads down. I look at Connor, his feet sealed to the second step, and perspiration dotting along his brow.

I swat at his arm, trying to get his attention without alerting our viewers to anything wrong. His eyes swing to me, but the blue depths are dulled and unfocused behind his black-rimmed glasses.

Are you okay? I mouth, my eyes roaming over his messy, blond hair.

His nod is slow, his throat working hard on a swallow as he drags his fingers through his hair. Connor is always pale, but right now, he's looking sickly. His veins are popping blue against his damp skin, and his top lip is gleaming with sweat.

Before I can make sure he's good, he begins to go down the stairs, the darkness slowly eating all of their forms. Sure, it feels ominous down here, but it's no different from any other place we've been. We just know more of the backstory here, and it'll be a first if an actual person was sealed inside the room, wasting away to nothing. It's a tortuous death.

I swallow down the concern I'm feeling and concentrate on the task at hand. We won't be rich if I don't pull up my big boy underwear and hype this shit up.

"As most of you know, this place housed one of the most heinous criminals of all time. Conroy Davies." I let the loud *thud* of my boots hitting the stairs echo as I draw the viewers in. "The story begins on a night when one of the worst hurricanes ravished the Florida coast. The power went down, and a few days later, the backup generators failed." Halfway down the stairs, I lose sight of the group, and the only indications I have of their presence are the small flashlight in Nick's hands and the sound of the meter ticking. "It's cold down here," I inform them. "The smell reminds me of damp clothing mixed with the smell of a recent rain shower." I put my hand out in front of me, the phone's light catching the engulfing blackness around its flash beam. I continue my story as I hit the next step. "The security locks couldn't stay engaged without power, and it gave Conroy the perfect opportunity, creating the perfect storm. He got out, killing the two men who attempted to hold him inside."

My feet reach the bottom and I find the others waiting for me, the meter still ticking out of control.

"It's getting worse," Mary whispers as her body trembles.

"This is just the beginning," Connor replies, his tone holding a heavy warning. He looks into the camera, his face solemn.

Whatever it is they're feeling has our audience on the edge of their seats, and I just know our bank accounts are going to be fat after this night.

It's just one night, and the money will be worth it.

"We have two choices," I tell our audience. "To the right"—I shine the camera down a long, winding corridor, both mine and Nick's flashlights doing little in the smothering darkness—"Or the left." I turn the other way and find a large, industrial door, the outside bolted shut. The screen ignites with comments as an overwhelming percentage demands we go to the left. "Let's get that rusted bolt open, guys." I chuckle at the enthused comments at the same time my stomach flips with trepidation.

Connor and Nick step forward, one with eagerness and the other with trepidation. Mary is holding the flashlight and the meter, both of them shaking as she stares at the guys working to move the large bolt.

"Do you think that's where they kept him?" She looks up at me just as the bolt screeches open, the noise jarring us both.

"Without a doubt."

Mary

The door opens on hinges that squeak in protest, the noise only adding to the mounting tension in the air.

Connor takes two large steps back, his shoulders straight as an arrow, the muscles vibrating with unease. Nick, the complete opposite, stands in the center of the doorway, peering down into the darkened corridor, his hand reaching backward, his fingers waving as he beckons for his flashlight.

I step forward on shaking legs and place the flashlight in his hand just as James moves up behind me, his scent comforting, but it's not enough to squelch the fear saturating my body.

"Shit," Nick curses as he steps into the corridor, shining his light back and forth. "This has to be it, guys."

The meter in my hands suddenly begins to make a whirring noise, the needle on the inside flicking back and forth quickly.

"What the hell?" I gasp.

I hold the meter closer to the door, only to hear a loud, resounding *crack* sound in the space around us.

"Did the meter break?" Connor asks, his voice shaking.

I look down at the device in my hand and find a large snaking crack in the glass, the needle laying precariously to one side.

"Do you see this, everyone?" James says excitedly. "The energy down here broke the EMF meter!"

27

"Th–th–is i–is dangerous," Connor stutters. "We shouldn't be down here."

James snickers as he looks down the darkened corridor, and that's when I realize Nick is no longer with us.

"Nick!" I scream as I drop the broken meter and run to the enormous doorway, squinting my eyes, praying they adjust to the dark quickly.

I'm pushed aside as Connor runs into the corridor screaming Nick's name. I turn around and find the fucking phone camera in my face as James is still filming, but his eyes are straining down the corridor.

"Turn it off!" I snap, pressing my palm into the camera. "Turn it off right now!"

James' thumb slides along the screen of his phone, and suddenly the light around us disappears. I scream in terror at the sudden black blanket that covers us, and I find myself climbing him like a tree.

"Mary." One of his hands cups the back of my head as the other wraps around my waist. My legs are wrapped around his hips and my arms are tight around his neck, my body shaking with fear. "Mary, I have you, it's okay."

His arm loosens from my waist as he turns on the flashlight app on his phone, and I tip my head up to look into his face. "I don't like it here, James," I confess.

"This one is it, Mary," he tells me as he smooths my curls back from my forehead. "We've made so much money already. It's just one night, and I promise to protect you." The warmth in his eyes is such a contrast to the chill surrounding us.

I want to believe him, and everything inside of me wants to give in to the emotion brimming in his irises, but I've had so many promises broken over the years. It's hard to trust anyone. I slip down from his arms and turn to look down the pitch-black corridor.

"We need to find them."

His hand is once again in mine, his large fingers slipping between my small ones, and then we step into the hallway. The constant *drip, drip* is the first noise I hear, and our shoes sound like we're stepping through puddles. James illuminates the floor at our feet, and that's when I notice a thin layer of green, moldy water standing along the floor's surface. Somewhere, there's a constant leak in this place, and the smell is atrocious.

We pass by open doorways, as large, steel structures with single windows in the frames stand ajar, illuminating the rooms with a single bed and a toilet. Some of the bedframes still have thin mattresses on them, and others are rusted and falling apart, but the farther we get down the hallway, the more things begin to look sinister.

There's a room that has hooks hanging from the ceiling, rusted, and the smell of iron permeates into the hallway. It looks like a room a butcher would use to hang his choice cuts of meat.

"What was this room for?" I ask James, my hand tightening in his, our palms sweating as we clasp tighter to one another.

"I don't know," he answers, moving the light from the room and shining it straight down the empty corridor ahead, still no sign of Nick or Connor.

"What happened down here?" I don't expect an answer. I know there isn't one. We will never know the horrors that took place at Bellgrove Park, a name so sweet sounding, but in actuality, a living hell.

The sound of chains or metal shaking filters through the corridor, and I stop, yanking on James' hand. Fear claws its way up my chest and stalling the air in my lungs. My heart crashes against my ribcage as my feet refuse to take another step. "Did you hear that?"

He stops and coasts the light back and forth, the loud, echoing sound continuing from just up the hall. I see the profile of his face as he turns to look at me over his shoulder, his nostrils flaring, and his jaw ticking with anxiety. "We need to find them."

My feet feel like lead as I drag them behind James, willing the courage I've had my entire life to somehow appear now that I need it the most. *I've endured worse,* I tell myself. This is no big deal. I've faced a monster every day for many years. I can endure a little noise in the dark.

We stop in front of another doorway, this one completely open, and when James shines the light into the room, we find instruments of torture lining the walls. Clamps, knives, chains, and different bondage straps.

"Oh God." My hand covers my mouth as bile threatens to spill from my throat.

The sound intensifies, emanating from this very room.

"Nick!" James calls out. "Are you in here, Connor?"

Neither answers his call and to my utter shock, James steps farther into the room.

"No." My voice quivers with terror as I try to haul him back. "We can't go in there."

"What if the noise is my brother? What if it's Connor? We can't leave them here." He sweeps his light ahead of us.

He's right, I know he's right, but my bowels are ready to let go at this point. I should have grabbed one of the large, industrial flashlights, and no matter how much I chastise myself right now, I made a grave error coming down here without one.

As the clanging metal gets louder, James moves his flashlight across the room, and there, sitting in a chair with an electrocution cap on his head is Nick. His body is vibrating, shaking the chair below it. His jaw is clenched so tight, and the whites of his eyes are bright throughout the dark room.

"Nick!" I scream as I run forward, releasing James' hand. "No, Nick!" James comes running up beside me just as I reach his brother, and I throw the cap off his head, my hands gripping his cheeks and turning his face toward me. "No, please."

His body continues to shudder as I feel the first tears slip down my cheeks.

"Did I get you?"

The sound of his voice has me pulling back, and I look into Nick's amused face. "Are you fucking kidding me?" Before I can even think my actions through, the palm of my hand claps against his cheek in a resounding smack that reverberates off the surrounding walls. "How could you do that to us?"

"It's just a joke, Mary." He hops down from the chair, his hand rubbing the cheek I slapped. "Jesus." Surprise is evident throughout his features, but there in the depths of his eyes is hurt. I've never slapped any of the guys before.

After knowing Nick for most of my life, I should be used to his antics, but each time, I want to kill him just a little bit more. He walks out of the room, his hand still rubbing his cheek, and I watch as he looks first to his left, in the direction we came from, and then to the right.

"Connor!" he calls out, his voice taking on a sharp edge of frustration. "Where are you?"

"You guys aren't together?" I snap as I circle around the room, looking for him.

"No, he went ahead," Nick says nonchalantly as he steps out into the hallway. "I think he went this way." He points to the right, then disappears into the darkness again.

"I hate him," I grit out, my teeth clenched with irritation as my body trembles with adrenalin.

"He's just trying to get a reaction out of you. You always give in." He lets out a chuckle, throwing my words back at me.

I'm in no mood to tolerate his snarkiness. I know he senses it when his hand slips back into mine and he guides us back out into the cold, wet hallway.

"Connor!" I hear Nick calling up ahead. "Where are you?"

We hurry up behind him, finding Nick standing in the center of the hallway, looking straight ahead, and as we get closer, we can see the outline of Connor a few feet ahead, staring at a large, steel door. The single window in the center has been blacked out with paint, and when James and I step up beside Nick, we notice the industrial door has been sealed shut.

"There are spray-painted words on here," Nick whispers, his words sounding reverent. "They've long faded and chipped away though. I can't tell what it says."

"Probably a warning not to open the door," James surmises with an excited look on his face.

Connor continues to stare straight ahead, his face still and his eyes wide as he murmurs, "He's still in there."

31

Connor

I'm frozen to the floor, unable to move any muscle of my body. The energy leaking from the room in front of me is the most sinister thing I've ever felt in my entire life. My skin erupts in goose bumps as the chill from the air grows more frigid and I can almost hear clawing against the metal of the door coming from behind that damn thing.

"We need to leave. Now," I say, even as my throat threatens to close. The fear running through me has set my entire system into flight mode. The years that have passed since the door was sealed have worn away at it. The cracks and rust have collected on it and paint chips peel away from its surface. I study it even as my brain is telling me to run. An orange-yellowish ooze runs from the cracks that have formed in the seal almost like blood leaking from the inside out.

James and Mary walk back upstairs to grab some equipment, while Nick and I stay planted in front of the door. I turn to follow them up, but Nick grabs me and draws my back up against his chest. The hold he has me in is very intimate and strange because while he has shown me affection with hugs, it's never been more than friendly. Being this close to someone has my brain starting to misfire.

"Don't be such a pussy, dude. We aren't leaving. You really need to lighten up," Nick replies, and I feel his hand come up and rub some of the tension away from the back of my neck, while his arm continues to hold me against him. "We are going to be okay. I promise," he whispers in my ear, sending a different kind of energy through me. Mary has always been our center, sure, but it hasn't stopped my mind from wandering to what it would be like to give in to the temptation that is Nick. The kiss he places on the back of my neck sends a jolt straight to my cock. The lust he brings out of me is borderline painful, but I've held onto my virginity this long. A little teasing won't break me. I want my first time to be romantic, so I guess I'm just a sappy pussy at this point.

"I'll protect you." His gentle tone eases me and effectively turns off my fear for just a second, but then a chilling breeze hits, bringing me back to our current situation. Nick releases me and walks up to the door to study it, using his fingers to scratch at the seal and it chips easily under his fingernails. "This will be easy enough to break away. A little elbow grease and we can crack this bad boy open," Nick says as the hairs on my arms stand on end.

"I really don't like this. Maybe we should leave this one alone. There's plenty of activity here that we don't need to do anything about this door." I try to sway him away from what feels like a place better left to the dead.

"No way. The money is pouring in from the viewers. We need to keep going," James says, coming up behind us with a tool bag he went upstairs to get. He pulls out a couple of chisel tools and passes one to Nick. When Nick accepts it, my heart drops as I watch on helplessly at them, knocking away at the seal containing an evil that should remain in there. Mary comes up beside me holding a flashlight and what looks like a file.

"You should see this. It's a picture taken of Conroy, and he looks exactly like you, Connor. It's kind of creepy," she says, passing me the photo to study. When this man's wicked eyes meet mine, it's like looking in a mirror at a completely different version of myself. My nerves kick into overdrive as I look back toward where this man was entombed and the overwhelming urge to rip them away from the door hits me. They've almost got the seal completely chipped off the door at this point.

"All right. I'm going to connect us back to the livestream and get this party started. You all ready?" James asks, standing up and wiping the sweat starting to drip from his forehead despite the cold temperatures down here.

"Not exactly," Mary mumbles beside me. I nod, agreeing with her, but James takes it as my compliance and taps away on his phone. The picture I'm still holding makes me feel like insects are crawling all over me. I look into the eyes of a madman in a picture, but it might as well be a mirror when it's a carbon copy of myself in the worn edges of the frame. Right down to the freckles dotting his nose.

"In three … two … one. Hey, Phantom Hood! We're back and we have quite the surprise for you! You all voted, and your curiosity has led us to the door of doom," James starts out, chuckling at his own joke. Mary and I just stare on helplessly as Nick chips the last of the seal away and reaches for the crowbar. James hands me the keys he found in the box of historical files about this place, and I just automatically know which key fits the fucking lock. It's vibrating with energy and begging for me to unleash the hell inside. Never has this happened before in my life and my fear I've been fighting through increases tenfold.

"You all get first access at Conroy Davies' cell and tomb with us. Viewer discretion is advised as we have no idea what we will find inside. As always, we leave disclaimers and warnings in our information tab for those that may be triggered by anything they witness during our investigations. If you're new here, I highly advise you to read over that before continuing viewing with us," James states quickly. I chuckle at his warning to the viewers, remembering with clarity the little old lady that got the shock of her life on our Bloody Bucket Bridge investigation. Poor lady tried to say we purposefully gave her a heart attack. It was her Karen review that ultimately sparked an explosion in our views, however, so I guess we have her to thank for our success so far.

"Connor?" James asks, drawing me back from my memories. I exhale heavily and reach out toward the lock with the key. When I finally wedge it past the rust and get it turned, a loud *clank* sounds and dust puffs out from under the door. Mary coughs and waves her hand to bat away the decades old smell assaulting us all.

"And here we go!" Nick says excitedly, wedging the crowbar into the crack of the door. All I can do is hope this doesn't come back to haunt us. Pun intended.

Nick

I grunt as Connor turns the handle and I push with all I have against the crowbar until the door finally gives way and flies open. Whispers start to fill the space around us, sounding unintelligible to our ears, but glancing over at Mary and seeing she has a recorder going tells me I'll be able to play this back and possibly get exactly what the dead are so eagerly trying to tell us.

"All right guys, for this time only, Mary is going to guide our path and show us inside. After this, it'll be night vision only as we don't want to miss anything that might be lurking in the dark," James says in a haunting way that creeps me the fuck out. But my humor is my armor.

"Hopefully it'll be a hot chick wanting to give out free ghost blowies," I crack back, earning a chuckle from James and a huff from Mary. I look behind me at Connor. He's standing there wide-eyed and unmoving, just staring into the darkness of the room.

"Come on, man. I got you," I say, holding out my hand for him to take. I know this shit has him off balance like he's never been before, but I'd let nothing happen to him or the rest of us. He puts his hand in mine, willingly telling me he's highly on edge. I look at Mary watching us and my heart almost jackhammers at the soft smile she gives me. She brings the light up to shine inside the room, and James heads through first to really give viewers the first look.

"Holy fuck, guys," he says in surprise, causing the rest of us to rush through. Nothing in my life ever prepared me for this moment however.

The room is scarce, with a desk and wooden chair tipped on its side with a leg missing, and a cot-like bed pushed up against the wall on the other side of the room. I'm a little stunned to find that the room looks rather clean and kept. There's no dust, even though it whooshed under the door when Connor unlocked it. There are no spiderwebs or even a smell coming from inside here. The dank air outside didn't even follow us in. It's like time stalled the day they sealed it shut. I try my hardest to process what's happening right now, but there's only one thing keeping my attention and the others'. It's what's on the bed that has us all captivated.

A skeleton lays there wrapped in a straitjacket and restraints from the bed it's on. There's some kind of cage-like contraption on its head even though the bottom jaw has long fallen and lies on the spinal cord of the neck.

"This must be the remains of Conroy Davies. He was left in this room and starved to death. The contraption you all see on his face was used to keep patients from biting or spitting on the orderlies. As you can see, he was left restrained to his bed. There are no signs of him struggling to get out and the restraints look almost brand new. The straps on his straitjacket have some nibble marks, possibly by rats, but otherwise untouched. This is the weirdest thing I've ever seen before in my life," James says, filling in the viewers. I watch as the phone lights up with a stream of comments and pings of funds being sent in. It's amazing to see how much this investigation is bringing in. We're going to be loaded by the time we leave in the morning.

A squeeze to my hand brings my attention back to Connor. I didn't even realize he was still clinging to me like a lifeline. My heart drops a little at his frozen stature. He's never been like this before.

"I can hear him," he whispers in a creepy as fuck voice, and chills erupt on my skin.

"The fuck are you talking about?" I ask, confused. Of course, James is talking. It's what he does best.

"Conroy. I can hear him. He wants me to come closer," Connor says a little louder this time, capturing James and Mary's attention. His eyes look almost black from his pupils expanding so far. James turns the phone on Connor and puts him front and center in the spotlight.

His glasses have fallen a bit, so I turn my back to James, blocking the viewers from seeing Connor like this. James can suck my dick as can the viewers because Connor is seriously starting to concern me.

"Hey. Focus on me, okay?" I tell him, pushing his glasses up his nose. The strongest urge to kiss the slight peppering of freckles across the bridge comes over me as I reassure him that everything's okay. I have no idea why I'm being so fucking protective of him right now. He blinks a couple of times and looks at me with wide eyes.

"I really don't like this," he whispers to me. I lean into him to tell him again it's going to be okay, but I'm interrupted by a dog barking.

"What the fuck? How'd a dog get in here? Don't move. Mary, don't leave him," I order, waving at James to follow me. He passes the phone to Mary, and she starts to speak to the fans as me and my brother run out of the room to find the mutt.

We spend the next thirty minutes searching in vain and find nothing as the mutt went silent when we started looking for it. With a dog being here, it could seriously implode the investigation because we won't know if we are capturing good footage or if it's Fido fucking about.

"Let's head back. We can leave out a can of tuna or something and set a trap for the furry asshole," James comments before heading back down toward the basement. I follow him and when we reach the bottom of the stairs, we jolt into a run, hearing Mary's soft cries coming from Conroy's room.

When we get inside, we find Connor lying beside the bed on the floor passed out, and Mary desperately trying to wake him up.

"What the fuck happened?" I ask her, dropping and putting my ear to his chest.

"I don't know! He looked almost possessed. He kept shuffling closer and closer to the bed while we were waiting on you guys to get back and then reached out to touch the corpse before his eyes rolled in the back of his head and he just dropped. I stopped the live feed," she says helplessly.

"It's okay. He must just be in shock. He'll be okay. Let's get back upstairs now," James orders, reaching down and plucking Mary up off the floor.

I check over Connor to make sure he didn't hurt himself in the fall. When he checks out, I look at James for directions.

"Come on. Let's get out of here. We've lingered too long. This room has a terrible vibe to it," he states, rubbing at his arms.

"No shit, dumbass. Connor literally kept saying that shit," I snap back at him before reaching under Connor. Somehow, the room feels less sinister than before and that concerns me to no end. Evil doesn't just up and leave.

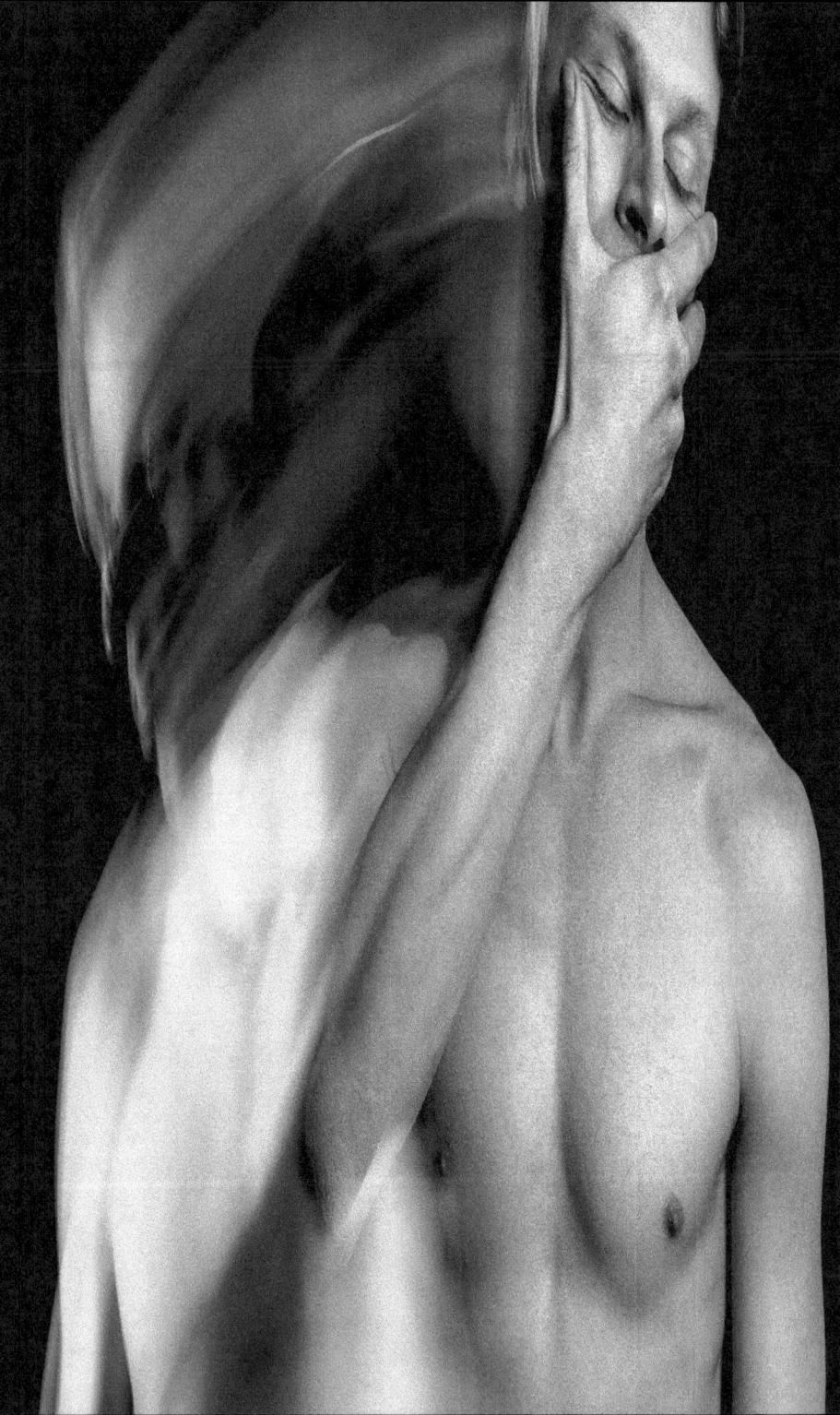

THREE

Mary

Nick grabs Connor under his arms and begins to drag him out of the room, his heavy breathing the only sound in the small confines of this room.

"There's no smell."

"Mary, let's get out of here." James grabs my hand, but I shrug him off.

"There's no smell of decay, almost like he never died. He's just sleeping."

"He's bare bones, Mary," James growls as he yanks on my arm. "He most definitely is dead."

The straitjacket has sunken in at the chest, the straps looking like they've been eaten away by rats, but the room itself is immaculate. No cobwebs, very little dust, and like I said, no smell.

"Why is it so clean in—"

James takes that moment to throw me over his shoulder and rushes us out of the room. My head pops up as we're storming by the lobotomy room, the electroshock room, and then the small cells for torture, but my eye stays trained on that sealed room, my heart beating out a quick staccato.

"James," I breathe out as he rounds the corner, heading back to the stairs. "He's still here."

"That's what Connor said too." James' heavy pants punctuate

each word as he rushes back up the stairs. "We're not going back down there."

At the top of the stairs, we find Nick on his ass with sweat dripping from his brow from the exertion of pulling Connor all this way. Connor lays still on the checkered floor, the gentle rise and fall of his chest the only indication he still lives.

James gently sets me back on my feet, his hand lightly brushing the hair off my forehead. I look up at him and find his honey eyes filled with worry.

"We should leave," Nick suggests as he stands, his worried eyes on Connor. I've always felt like there was more of a connection between them than the rest of us.

"Listen…" James holds up his hands as he speaks. "I don't want to be here either, but look at this."

He holds out his phone to show us the PayPal and Venmo accounts, and Nick curses loudly.

"That many zeros?"

"It's a lot of money," I whisper.

"If we leave, they will demand we give it back. This is the most we've ever made." His eyes skip down to Connor. "Let's try to get him up and comfortable on his cot. He was just freaked out is all."

I drop to my knees, then fall forward onto my hands, crawling toward Connor. He does look like he's peacefully sleeping, his breathing even and strong. I place my hand on his forehead and gasp at how cold his skin is.

"He's freezing."

James and Nick both come forward and do the same, then give each other a look.

"He feels normal to me," Nick mutters.

"Same," James adds.

"He needs his bed and a blanket." I rush to my feet and run over to the area we claimed as our sleeping quarters. The fingers that touched Connor's skin are grasped into a fist, the chill still emanating from their tips.

40

I pull apart our cots and set them up as we usually do. James, Nick, me, then Connor. It's been like this since we first started, and even before we began this journey of phantom chasing, we would line our sleeping bags in the same formation at our houses for sleepovers. I find our pillows and blankets in one bag as Nick and James both carry an unconscious Connor to his cot.

"He needs to be warmed up," I growl as I grab his blanket.

"He doesn't feel cold, Mary," Nick huffs as they lay Connor down.

As soon as Connor's body hits the cot, he groans something unintelligible and turns onto his side, cuddling his blanket to his chest.

"He's just had a fright," James murmurs. "He'll come around in a bit."

"I'm going to finish with these lasers." Nick heads over to the machines he knows best as James sits on his cot.

"People are wondering why we're not going live."

"We can set it up and talk about this place for a bit, then leave it live as we sleep. People love being fucking creepers," Nick calls out.

"How do you feel about that?" James asks me. He's always been receptive to how I'm feeling, and right now, the thought of anyone watching me sleep is giving me the creeps. I had enough of that growing up.

But we don't have a choice, and I knew what this was all about when I agreed to join them.

"It's fine. We have to do it to keep that money." My teeth sink into my bottom lip as I watch Connor shift on the cot.

As Nick and James talk animatedly into the camera about the past horrors of this place, I lay on my cot and watch Connor. He moves now and then, but he's mumbling a lot. Sometimes I catch my name or Nick's.

I reach my hand toward his cot, my fingers itching to smooth out the crinkle between his brows when his eyes snap open and stare straight at me. His blue eyes look so dark, like they're nearly black, his pupils almost completely blown out.

"Connor?" I whisper, not wanting to attract the attention of the others.

His full lips curl upward into a slow grin as he reaches his hand out to grasp my fingers, the frigid feel of them making me flinch.

"Are you cold?"

"Are you offering to come over here and warm me up, little lady?" His tongue flicks out against his teeth, and I feel my cheeks warm with his words. Connor flirts with me, but it's never this forward. "You really are such a little thing, aren't you?"

His icy fingers grip mine as his darkened eyes feasts along my body, making me simultaneously hot and apprehensive. Connor is the shy one of the group, and even though he's shown me attention often, he's not one to be this confident in his flirtations.

"That's it for tonight," Nick says to the camera, making Connor release my hand. "We'll leave this running in case you feel brave enough to see what happens while we sleep."

James chuckles as he sets up the camera onto the tripod, then his eyes skim over to me and Connor, softening when our gazes meet. James has a dark energy that reminds me of *him*, and it confuses me when my body craves his looks and touches. I shouldn't want that from someone who reminds me of the man who took without asking for years.

But I do.

My eyes slip away from his heated look and land once again on Connor, once again in deep slumber. His actions confuse me, but I liked them. I liked a more take charge, Connor. It's a secret desire of mine, to be pursued, preyed upon, then captured.

My stomach warms as my heart dips. I'm a filthy whore who likes to be forced, and it's something I've endured throughout the years. My body enjoys it while my mind is ashamed and screaming for it to stop.

As the guys settle into bed, I watch the laser beams shooting straight along the walls, waiting for the moment one flickers, even in the slightest. I hate when everything falls dark and silent, leaving me with haunting memories of fear and anticipation.

My hearing perks up, listening for the sounds of socked feet hitting the shag carpeting just outside my bedroom door, for the squeak of the hinges as my door opens, and then the cloying scent of whiskey as he steps into the room.

I slam my eyes shut, forcing the memory to recede as echoes of the lasers dance behind my eyelids. I force myself to ignore the twisting of my stomach as it threatens to expel my dinner, and I ignore how my panties grow warm with the thought, once again showering me in shame.

I gather the blanket closer to my chest as the cold air stings the skin of my cheeks. A groan escapes me as I imagine my uncle turning down the heat to save money, leaving me and my cousins to freeze with our threadbare blankets.

Then reality slowly seeps back to me, and I snap my eyes open, forcing them to adjust quickly to the dark. It's too dark.

I sit up and notice the lasers are off, including the light on the camera. Everything is shut down as if the generators gave out. Only they wouldn't go out, they're gas run, and we filled them up before getting here.

The hairs along my arms stand up as I swing my legs over the side of my cot, my eyes landing on Connor's still form. He's sleeping, and when I look over my shoulder, I find Nick spread eagle on his bed, his arms hanging over the edges. James is on his stomach with his hands tucked under his pillow.

They look so peaceful. I really feel bad for waking them up, but something is wrong. I open my mouth to call Nick when something catches my attention over by the large desk. It's about ten feet in front of our cots, and right now, there's something—*or someone*—sitting in the chair. It slowly spins around, and I see the outline of a female's body, but that's not the shocking part.

She's holding her fucking head.

"I'm dreaming." My words are coarse. "I'm fucking dreaming."

"Mary," the headless secretary says as she stands, the silver aura shining brightly around her distorting her features. "You need to leave this place—"

Suddenly, she flies across the room, seemingly being sucked toward the stairs, and her hollow screams echo around the room as I suck in a breath, readying myself to scream as well.

A hard, cold slap lands on my face as something frigid seals around my mouth. My scream hits a barrier, effectively sealing off any attempt to alert the guys sleeping peacefully beside me.

I'm shoved back onto the cot, my head hitting the pillow with a *swoosh* as something heavy settles on my legs and stomach. I can't see anything through the darkness of the room, but I can *feel* it.

The rub of something very familiar along the inside of my thigh, the squeezing pressure of fingers digging into my cheeks, and a panting breath of arousal as it ricochets off my throat, only this time it's sub-zero instead of warm.

I have to be fucking dreaming.

My mouth is released, and I open it to suck in a breath, only to have it filled in the next second with something cold and wet. Something is kissing me. No. *Someone* is kissing me, nibbling along my lips, and dragging a frigid breath along my cheek to settle at the shell of my ear.

"You really are such a little thing, aren't you?"

"Connor?" I whisper into the dark, but I know it's not him, even if he did utter those exact words earlier.

Cold fingers dig into the waistband of my leggings, hauling the material down to my thighs as an icy wet tongue slips inside my ear. Shock courses through me, stalling any reactions I have, and the crisp temperatures around me make my thoughts and movements sluggish.

"How tight are you?"

The voice sounds like it's garbled, the words spoken as if underwater, and when glacier tendrils slip over my mound and into my folds, a vision springs in front of me in perfect clarity.

I'm thrusted into my childhood room, the stench of stale whiskey saturating my senses, and fingers gripping the waistband of my underwear.

"How tight are you, my sweet Mary?"

"No, Uncle, please. Not tonight."

A hard slap yanks me out of my past and right back into the present as long icicles penetrate my core, another pressing into my clit.

"You're here with me now." The eerie voice hits my ear. "You will know who's fucking you, and this time when you come, it'll be me you'll see."

I don't see anything in front of me, but I feel the presence on top of me and inside of me as my senses still swim with the scent of whiskey.

My pants are ripped off in a cold rush of energy, and a whimper escapes me as I slowly come to my senses.

I'm not dreaming.

The guys' soft snoring is filtering through the air around me, and I feel as though I'm stuck to the bed in paralysis, unable to stop what's already begun. Fear coats me as my breathing picks up, the quick pants heightening the terror that's slowly drowning me.

"No," I moan as those icy-cold fingers spread me open, still pressing against my clit.

A barrier is slapped back over my mouth when Connor turns over in bed, his eyes slowly blinking into focus. He looks confused as I stare at him wide-eyed, but of course, he sees nothing on top of me.

My legs are spread open farther, and then it feels like I'm being ripped in two as something thick is slowly pushed inside of me, inch by agonizing inch.

A wintery breath is exhaled over my face as whatever it is begins to move in and out of me, my mind reeling as my pussy tightens.

Connor turns around, his back now facing me as I continue

to be defiled by an invisible man. I shake my head, trying to dislodge whatever it is over my mouth, but a chuckle sounds around me at the effort.

"I'm going to make you come all over my fat cock, and you're going to cry pretty tears for me as you do it. I want you to feel every inch of me ripping you open, sweet little girl."

As this *thing* fucks me into the thin cot, ice is pressed to my clit, dragging a pain-filled moan from my throat. It doesn't feel bad, and shame rears its ugly head, my constant companion. I feel my hips lift off the bed, changing the angle of the thrusts, helping them hit a little deeper. The pressure on my clit intensifies, making my pussy clench, and driving the thing above me to fuck me harder.

I'm wet, sopping, fucking wet, and nothing but shame courses through me as I feel the telltale signs of my orgasm.

"This little pussy is going to milk my cock, isn't it?"

The coil in my lower belly tightens as I try my darndest to fight it. My neck lengthens as I tip my head back, tears indeed slipping down my cheeks, just like he said they would.

"Come for me, little girl. Conroy loves when little girls squeeze his cock dry."

Conroy?

Conroy Davies?

Just as the harrowing truth hits me full force, my pussy tightens and erupts in waves of sensation, the euphoria dragging me into the pits of shameful pleasure. My hips jerk against an unseen force, and the cock inside of me gives one last thrust, then I feel it pulse with its release, the warmth of it a surprising contrast to the cold of its shaft.

I've just been raped by a serial killing ghost, and I didn't hate it.

Connor

I jolt awake as the most sinister dream I've ever experienced leaves me. I could almost feel myself chopping off the receptionist's head, and I've never been more disgusted in my life. Her haunting scream was cut short, though it's still ringing in my ears. I pat around the bed, trying to find my glasses, and when I do, I put them on and breathe out a sigh of relief.

I look around and find everyone sleeping. Mary is snoozing on the cot beside me, bundled in on herself like she's trying to protect herself from some unseen force. Her form is a blurry blob but I can make out who it is by her small frame. The feeling of having her lying beside me takes away some of the sickness I feel from the dream. I sit up and rub the sleep from my eyes, trying to remember how the fuck I got here. The last thing I remember was being in that god-awful basement in Conroy's room. Just as I think about it, a deep, cackling laugh fills the space we're in, and my heart pounds out of my chest.

Looking around, I see they set up a livesteam before passing out, but it looks like it's been cut. I can't see shit, everything is pitch-black around me. The laugh sounds again and my spine tingles with fear. A shadow forms in front of me and I shout as a perfect form of myself appears with the evilest smile I've ever seen. No one is waking up, and it sets off all kinds of internal alarms inside me.

"Look at you. So soft, so sensitive. You know how long I've been waiting to get out of that fucking prison?" The thing in front of me speaks and slowly tilts its head like it's studying me. His form flickers a bit, but otherwise remains incorporeal, and my brain takes a toll on itself, trying to understand the entity in front of me.

"What are you?" I try to muster up as much courage as I can as I reply. My need to run and get the fuck away from this spirit is strong. He's radiating so much evil. My body is having a hard time staying put, but if I move, he will have open access to Mary.

"I think you know, little boy. Ask the right question. Who... am I?" He pauses a bit before he finishes. He stays in the same position, squatted down in front of me with his head tilted and a sinister smile lighting his face as he waits for my reply. There's no doubt I'm looking at and speaking to Conroy right now, and it's our fault he was released from that room.

"How about this? What do you want?" I ask instead, slowly moving to try to shield Mary from him.

"Don't worry about that, boy. I've had a taste of that pussy and it is quite a delight. You should give it a ride," he says, nodding toward Mary. Rage fills me at the thought of his vile hands on her, but before I can act on my violence, my limbs freeze. I feel my hand lift of its own volition, and I slap myself across the face unwillingly.

"You're mine, little boy. The perfect puppet for me. I control you, and I think it's time to have some fun," he tells me before erupting into a cloud of smoke. Little tentacles spread out as I watch on in horror as they caress my face and start filling my nose and mouth. I choke and gag at the shadows invading me, but I'm fucking helpless to stop it.

I momentarily black out from the experience, but when I come to, the only thing I'm in control of is watching helplessly as my body stands and stretches. I can feel everything, yet I can't control anything.

"Watch and learn, little boy. I'll show you how to use this wasted flesh properly," I feel myself say, yet it's not me. The voice is mine, but it's not me speaking. This can't be happening right now. I can't wake from this nightmare and warn the others because I have zero control over what's happening with my body. I'm me, yet I'm Not Me.

Not Me walks over to one tote we brought in and grabs out rope and duct tape. My mind buzzes with fear as I try desperately to fight against this thing inside me. It's fucking useless. I can't do anything. I feel Not Me chuckle at my wasted attempts to take back control. Not Me stands and walks over to James first, tying up his legs and arms on the cot he's sleeping on, then gently taping his mouth. He never moves or twitches. This has to be a dream. Why aren't they waking up if it isn't a dream? Not Me then stands and walks over to Nick to repeat the process of what Not Me did to James.

Once Not Me is finished double-checking the knots and ensuring they aren't going anywhere, Not Me slaps Nick until he's awake and staring at me like I've lost my mind. Unfortunately, I have, and there's nothing I can do to stop this. Not Me stands and does the same thing to James as Nick fights like a demon to escape. Both of them are shouting muffled, intelligible things, and I feel Not Me laugh out loud.

Not Me walks back over to Nick as he thrashes against the rope holding him to the cot. Not Me reaches out and grabs onto Nick's dick right through his pants. Nick stills and stares at me with wide eyes, and I almost want to fucking cry at the confused look on his face.

"I can see all the thoughts and memories you have. You've wanted this man for a while now, you naughty little boy. Let me help you out," Not Me says, and Nick rears his head back against his pillow like I've grown a second head. I really fucking have.

I feel as Not Me massages Nick's length until he's steel in my hand. Nick groans and withers on the cot. I can make out the muffled *'Stop, Connor'* but I'm as helpless to this as he is. His head jolts back, and somehow I just know he's about to cum, but I feel Not Me stop and spares a glance in James' direction to find him watching us with rapt attention. His cock is straining in his jeans, and I feel Not Me chuckle, whereas I'm horrified and confused by my actions, and James' reaction to me assaulting his brother. My head is a jumbled mess in this dream unfolding.

"Poor little boys. I really appreciate you letting me out to play. It's been so, so long. Do you have any idea how loud silence can be? I need some sweet screams to refuel me. I also found a secret you fuckers are going to love. Watch this," Not Me tells them as I let go of Nick and stand.

I watch in horror as Not Me turns toward my cot and Mary's still sleeping form. The guys sound like they are fighting harder than before and cursing up a storm behind the duct tape on their mouths. Not Me walks over to the cot, and I feel as I caress her leg and side. She sighs with contentment and starts to release herself from the bundled position she's in.

Not Me stands and undresses as the guys scream behind the tape still covering their mouths. Once I'm completely naked and horrified, terror fills my mind as Not Me reaches out and pulls the blanket off of Mary. Even with how gentle Not Me is being, it somehow makes me feel more sickened with what Not Me is doing. She's already naked from the waist down, and my heart pumps at the sight.

Mary never stirs as she lays there, as naked as I am, and so fucking beautiful it almost hurts. This has to be a sick dream though. There's no other explanation for it. Not Me kneels on the bed and opens her legs before bending over and licking her pink slit. Her taste explodes in my mouth, and I feel Not Me groan, even while my own mind does the same. Fuck, this is so goddamn wrong. She's never going to forgive me if she learns about this. Of what I'm doing to her and the guys.

Not Me drops down completely on the cot and grips her legs in a stronghold as we suck her clit into my mouth and Mary wakes with a groan, grinding her pussy all over my face. When she finally comes to and realizes what's happening, a look of horror crosses her features. Her hips still and I can't do anything but watch as the horror story I'm being forced into playing out unravels.

"Connor! What the hell are you doing!?!" she demands, fighting to get away from me. I feel Not Me tighten the grip I have on her legs to the point I know she's going to have bruises from it. She shoves at my head and fights to get away, but Not Me won't let go. Not Me continues to lick and suck at her. I feel helpless and violated even as Not Me continues to force this on her.

My cock fills quickly the more she fights, disturbing me further. Not Me finally picks my head up and starts crawling up Mary's body, gripping her by the throat with one hand to pin her down. The sensations assaulting me are so foreign and unusual as I feel Not Me guide my length through her soaking wetness. I'm not an expert on sex, but something tells me this isn't a normal reaction for a woman to have if she were in this situation.

Not Me lifts one of her legs until her knee is resting on the crook of my arm and guides my tip inside of her. She fights harder to get away from me as she claws at my chest. The pain of her scratches only makes the pleasure I feel multiply as Not Me slowly starts to enter her. Her pussy ripples around me, and I find myself groaning in pleasure as Not Me lets it slip from my mouth. This bastard really is a sick fuck.

"Now the fun part," Not Me says before slamming me the rest of the way inside her. Mary screams and then groans. Her pussy feels like heaven. Even as disgusted as I am with what's happening, the pleasure consuming me makes that feeling take a backseat as I helplessly ride this out.

"Connor," Mary whimpers, and Not Me chuckles.

"Not Connor, little girl, although he's very much here and enjoying this as much as I am," Not Me replies, and I see Mary's features harden. Not Me starts to pound into her as she tries so hard to hold back moans I know she wants to let free. Not Me pulls free of her and tosses her to the floor in front of James and Nick's cots. She looks like she's pinned down by some invisible force, face down and ass high in the air. Not Me crawls toward her, glancing quickly at James and Nick.

James' cot is on its side like he tipped over from fighting to get free. They're both still yelling behind their taped mouths and fighting like hell to save Mary from this. From *me*.

Not Me grips Mary's hips and guides my length back inside her sweet walls that clutch me in a vise-like hold.

"Show them, little girl. Show them you love it when it's taken from you. Come on my cock," Not Me orders her, and I pull back before slamming inside her. She lets loose a hoarse cry as Not Me pounds her from behind. I must be just as equally as sick as Conroy because having her beneath me like this on her hands and knees, pinned and taking my cock so good fills me with a high I never thought possible.

Tingles erupt at the base of my spine, and my balls draw up. Mary's moaning loudly now and somehow getting wetter than before. Her pussy sucks me in, and before I understand the pleasure she's feeling, or the pleasure I'm feeling, her walls clamp down on my cock as she screams out, and I helplessly shout as I feel my length start to pulse inside her with my release.

"That, little boys, is how you make this pretty little thing come undone." I feel Not Me say as Not Me glances up to find James and Nick statue still and watching with lust and desire coating their features.

Not Me laughs sinisterly as my own mind loses its fight to stay awake. I feel Not Me withdraw from Mary, and she falls to the floor, cradling in on herself just as she was on the cot, and Conroy's words about having her before hit me full-force. I'll find a way to get this sick son of a bitch back inside that cell if it's the last thing I do.

James

The sunlight scorches through my eyelids as it slips through the cracks of the boarded-up windows. My body aches from the thin as fuck cots, and I reach my arms over my head to stretch. One eye cracks open and I look to my right to find Nick still fast asleep, his hands tucked under his cheek like a sweet angel.

Far fucking from it.

Mary is asleep on her cot between Nick and Connor. Only Connor's cot is empty. I sit up slowly and look around the room. It's chilly in the early morning, but that's not the only thing standing out. The generators have shut off. Nothing is running. No lasers and our livestream has been turned off.

My socked feet hit the cold floor as I search for my boots. They should be right here. This is where I left them last night. I locate my boots strewn under Nick's cot, and my brows crinkle in confusion.

I feel like I'm missing something.

Last night was one of the most restful nights of my life. I don't even remember dreaming, and the fact that all of us slept so soundly means there's something more at play here.

There's something inside of me that's screaming to find Connor. So I let my brother and Mary sleep as I go in search of him. I get to the stairs and look up, but my feet descend like I already know where I'll find him. It's an eerie feeling, the way this basement's cold, musty scent envelops me, at the same time, pushing me onward.

The hairs along my arms raise as goose bumps break out on my skin. This place is sinister, and I'm more than ready to go. I just want everyone in the same room first so we can pack up and leave.

Conroy's cell is straight ahead, the door still wide open, and just as dark as it was last night. There's no light down here, and as I pass each room, a buzzing noise grows louder. The energy in this place is filled with nefarious intent. The souls trapped here are either angry or insane.

Or both, like Conroy.

Silence immediately falls when I step into Conroy's cell, and I stumble back at the sight in front of me. Connor is laying on the small cot, the skeleton shoved to the floor, and he's as naked as the day he was born. Something nags at my subconscious, like I'm forgetting something, but I can't quite put my finger on it.

"Connor," I hiss, confusion still swimming through my mind. "Wake up."

A low growl permeates the silence, and I stiffen at the sound. I watch as Connor's arms stretch over his head, and then he slowly turns toward me, a lazy smile on his lips.

"Jane," he says with a chuckle. "It's only James. Come on out, little girl."

The tone of his voice is off, like it's Connor, but at the same time, not him. I don't know what to make of the situation until a scruffy-looking dog sticks its head out from under the bed.

"Nick has always wanted a dog," Connor says as he stands, his fully naked body on display, along with the massive boner he's sporting. "I bet he'll be happy I found her."

"Why are you down here?" My eyes don't leave the dog as it emerges from under the bed. "Why are you sleeping on this bed, and why is his body on the floor?"

The dog looks like it's been shoved into a dryer without a cling-free sheet, and now it's brownish fur is standing in clumps on end. The tufts around its ears are sparse as if it's been scratching them constantly with its long nails.

I think it's some kind of Lab or Retriever.

"It's not like he needs them. The bed or the body." He gives me a wink as he strides by, whistling for the mangy dog to follow him.

As the dog passes, it snaps at me, a low growl slipping from its toothy mouth, but then it chases after Connor, its scraggly tail wagging happily. We need to get out of this place.

I meet Connor at the top of the stairs, his hands on his hips as he looks around. "We should start up the generators."

"Nah, no point," I tell him. "We're leaving. Can you get some clothes on?"

"Oh, we can't leave," he says matter-of-factly. "The doors are all sealed."

"What do you mean?" I'm not fully paying attention as my eye stays on the dog, and Connor doesn't bother to explain.

The dog is sniffing around the receptionist's desk, and then I gape as it squats to piss beside the chair, its mouth open on a pant, almost looking like it's laughing. The dog is fucking looney too. The way its wiry brown fur stands on end and the patches throughout its body tells me it's been here a long time.

She comes up behind me as I head to the cots, her nose sniffing along my pants. "We're not keeping the dog."

Connor finally finishes dressing as Nick groans awake. "Dog?" he croaks out as he struggles to sit up. "Dude! You found the dog!" he exclaims, his face beaming with excitement.

Why does it feel like we're missing something?

The commotion makes Mary stir, and when she opens her eyes, anguish is shining in their depths. Then it hits me. I had a terrible dream, one where Mary was defiled by Connor, while Nick and I had no other choice but to watch. I feel ashamed, and I can't quite bring myself to look her in the eyes.

"We're leaving." I snap my fingers. "Let's get up and pack this place up."

"No can do." Connor shakes his head, and that's when I notice he doesn't have his glasses on. He's usually blind without them.

"Where are your glasses?"

"I don't know." He shrugs, no expression on his face as Mary sits up.

"I want to go home," she mutters, her eyes firmly on her hands in her lap and her mouth turned downward.

"The doors won't open," Connor states with exasperation. "We can't leave."

"What?" I ask, finally absorbing what he's saying. "What do you mean?"

"Nick, want to go check the children's ward?" He nudges my

brother, a mischievous look on his face. "Jane came out of there this morning."

"We're naming the puppy Jane?" Nick snickers as he rubs her wiry head. Her tongue is lolling out of the side of her mouth and her eyes are hooded with contentment. So she likes everyone else but me.

"Well, we already have a Mary." Connor winks at Mary, but she doesn't respond. If anything, she looks sicker than she did a moment ago and her eyes haven't budged from her lap. Jane senses her distress and whines, her eyes on Mary.

"Mary and Jane." Nick chuckles as he reaches his fist toward Connor for a bump.

I make my way to the door, not liking what Connor is saying about being trapped in here, none of this feels as nonchalantly as he's making it sound.

My hand wraps around the elongated handle, and when I press on it, the thing doesn't budge. I bear all my weight down onto it and let a string of curses loose when the thing barely moves.

"Nick!" I call. "Get over here."

He comes over, running his hand through his hair, and giving me a lazy grin. "What's up?"

"The doors aren't opening."

"What?" He sidles up beside me before focusing on the door. "Move out of the way."

"If I can't do it, what makes you think you can?"

I move for him, then watch as he struggles with the door, his feet lifting off the ground as he bears down.

"We're trapped!" he screams with fear, the sound like nails on a chalkboard.

"What?" Mary appears around the corner, her blanket still wrapped around her shoulders. "No, I can't stay here any longer. Something is wrong here."

The agony in her eyes is setting my heart at a rapid beat. Her words are whispered but each word is punctuated with panic, and she's folding in on herself, the blanket effectively hiding everything but her head. She's right, something is here lurking with us, and now it's making sure we can't leave.

"Nick," Connor calls out as he heads to the staircase. "Let them figure it out. I want to show you something in the children's ward."

"Why isn't he worried?" I mumble under my breath, watching as Connor hits the stairs, taking two at a time, the scraggly mutt not too far behind him.

"Maybe he's finally done with being worried? I mean, it's not like anything will change even if he is worried. Then again, he almost had a heart attack in the basement yesterday."

Nick dusts off his hands and follows Connor, his messy hair bouncing with his steps.

"Are you cold?" I give Mary a once-over, noticing her body trembling. I hate seeing her like this.

"I can't find my clothes," she whispers as her eyes fill with tears. "I need to leave."

"You can't find your clothes?" Again, something is nagging at the back of my mind, like a memory trying to resurface.

"I think I took them off in the middle of the night." She begins to tremble in her blanket, which makes sense if she doesn't have anything on underneath it.

The uncertainty is shining blatantly from her eyes as she looks over her shoulder toward the desk.

"Maybe we can break some windows," I murmur because I'm starting to feel frantic now about being locked in this place for more than one night. "I'm going to sue the owner when we get out of here."

"*If* we get out of here." Mary sniffles as she heads back to the cots.

"I have extra clothes in my bag." I nod toward my cot. "Grab them."

"I don't want to spend another night here," she says, her voice saturated with terror as she digs through my bag. "I won't survive."

FOUR
Mary

While James rifles through our tool case, in search of something to break down the door or windows, I dress in his too-large hoodie and track pants. I roll the waistband a few times to make them more secure.

I don't know where my clothes are, but I have a feeling they didn't just magically disappear. We're all having a hard time looking at each other this morning, all except Connor. They're talking about their dreams being vividly detailed last night, and I would've thought so too if my thighs weren't soaked in cum, and my vagina throbbing with sharp pain.

I was defiled by Connor, and something else entirely inconceivable.

Connor was also defiled last night. I know it.

My hand slaps over my mouth as a sob works its way up my throat. My bladder is screaming for release, and I don't want to seek out a bathroom alone in this creepy place.

"James?" I call out after taking in a deep breath and lowering my hand back down to wrap around my waist.

"Yeah?" he answers, something heavy hitting the floor before he appears around the corner, his eyes filled with worry.

"Could you come with me to find a bathroom?"

"Oh," he says, his throat working on a swallow. "There's

one on this floor. Obviously, it's not flushing or anything, but it's not disgusting. Unless you need to do a number two, in that case, we might have to think of—"

"Just number one," I cut him off with a small smile as I grab up my tissue pack. "Thankfully."

He leads me to a door just beyond the receptionist's desk, my eyes lingering on the dark, wood surface as we pass. There's something about that area and its lure over me. I want to sit in the chair, wipe the dust off the receiver-less rotary phone, and open up the romance novel stashed in the bottom right drawer. The familiarity I have with the desk is jarring. James opens the door and I peer inside, finding a fairly clean room.

"Thank you," I whisper as I step in.

"I'll wait out here," he replies as I shut the door.

There are two small stalls, so I head to the one next to the wall and surprisingly find there's a clean toilet. It has no water, obviously, but the bowl is fairly clean, save for the layer of dust coating every surface. I do my business and wince as more pain radiates from between my legs. It's a familiar ache, one I've dealt with for most of my adolescence. I never thought this pain would ever happen again.

I was raped last night.

I know it's the truth. I just don't know how it happened, or the entire story, but I do know the guys don't remember anything, or if they do, they think it to be remnants of a dream.

Maybe that's how Conroy wanted it. He wanted me to remember what happened in some sick way of keeping him in my mind.

I choke on a sob as I wipe myself, the pain intensifying with the action. I really can't stay here another night. I won't survive.

As soon as I'm finished, I step from the stall, and the sight in front of me has a scream wrenching from my throat. James flies in through the door and grabs my face in his hands.

"Mary, what is it?"

I point to the counter with the single sink in the center, unable to utter a word. He follows my finger and then a curse growls from his throat.

"Are those…"

"My clothes," I choke out. "My clothes are in a bathroom I have never used."

He slowly approaches the sink as I stand behind him, waiting to see what he discovers, and when another curse grinds from his mouth, I know it's bad.

"What?"

"They have something on them," he says.

"What is it?"

"I think it's … cum."

"What?" I screech. "From who?"

"A person who can shoot glow in the dark swimmers."

"James, I swear to God—"

"Seriously!" He holds up my tank top, showing me the disgusting things all over it. "Look at it."

It looks like someone broke open a glow stick and smeared its contents on my tank top.

"It can't be cum."

He brings the shirt up to his nose and takes a whiff, his face immediately cringing.

"I promise you it is."

"How? From whom?" My lips begin to tremble and as soon as he sees it, he drops my shirt to the floor, and gathers me in his arms, his lips pressing against the top of my head. "I'm scared."

"Me too," he whispers.

Nick

Something is up with Connor today. I follow him to the children's ward with Jane nipping at his heels while he whistles a haunting tune I've never heard before. Something is just up today, period. I try too hard to remember last night because something is telling me shit went down, and the man walking in front of me is responsible for it.

"How are you making it around without your glasses?" I question him. Connor is as blind as a bat without them. He pauses his whistling and chuckles, something wholly unlike him. Connor is more of a giggle man, not a sassy chuckle dude. I know his giggles damn it and this isn't his.

"Got perfect vision right now, and I really like what I'm seeing," he replies, turning his head and looking me dead in the eyes. I rear back like I've been slapped. He's never been a fucking flirt.

"Don't you think it's weird we're locked in here like this right now?" I question him again, trying to get any kind of reaction out of him other than carefree. He just chuckles again and turns to keep walking like he knows exactly how to navigate this place.

Jane barks out excitedly and follows him like they've known each other for years. I shake my head and keep following him, pulling out the piece of paper I shoved in my pants pocket last night before going down to Conroy's cell. We're on some kind of breezeway right now passing through from the main building to get to the ward and the windows are busted out. They still have bars on them, though, but the sunshine coming through provides plenty of light for me to see.

When I flatten the sheet, I try not to give any reaction to what I'm reading to alert Connor because the first thing that stands out on Conroy's patient profile is that he loves to whistle when he's in a good mood. He tends to draw when he's mad. The reality hits me and I want to fucking lose my shit, but I have to keep a level head right now.

When we get to the doors on the other end of the breezeway, I shove the paper back into my pocket to help Connor with the double doors. We're both pressed against them, shoving hard, and finally, it gives way from decades of neglect. The smell of rotten wood hits me instantly and I cringe, whereas Connor inhales deeply, his smile big and sinister.

"Well, hello, dearies. Daddy's home," he mutters and walks forward. There's no doubt left inside me. This is Conroy's spirit possessing Connor right now.

When we make it to a giant playroom area littered with old toys, I stop to think about why he's brought me to this wing.

"I want to talk to Connor," I demand when my mind can't take it anymore. He freezes and turns toward me, smiling widely again.

"So you figured it out, you smart little cookie. Too bad Connor isn't here right now. He's weak and pathetic anyway." This motherfucker shrugs like it's no big deal.

"You're wrong. He's the strongest one of us all," I declare, but it just earns me another chuckle from the thing in front of me wearing my best friend's body. My own body is vibrating with a mix of rage and helplessness. Any other time or person I would have delivered an uppercut from Satan's right hand over those kinds of comments about someone I love.

"If that were the case, then why can't he fight me off? It seems we're one and the same."

"Bullshit! Connor's nothing like you! He's sweet and gentle!" I take a step forward but this situation is so goddamn conflicting because that's my best friend and almost lover in front of me. I'd never hurt him, but that thing possessing him... I'd resurrect the motherfucker just to slaughter him myself.

"Poor little boy wants his lover back. Fine. You can have thirty minutes. I'm growing tired of driving this bag of flesh," Conroy replies before his eyes roll to the back of his head and he drops to the floor like he's passed out.

I rush over to him quickly as he blinks and then squints. He grabs his head, groaning, and then horror fills his features.

"Oh fuck! Nick! You have to get the others and get the fuck out of here! Leave me right now and get them out!" he screams hysterically. I grab his face in my hands, helping him sit up, and just kiss him to shut him up. I'm scared, he's scared, fuck we're all scared, but I can't resist holding back with him anymore.

63

I pull away after a long moment, looking him in his eyes while keeping my hands on his face. "Listen to me. We're going to figure this out, okay? I'm not leaving you, nor are we going to let this motherfucking ghost keep fucking with us," I reassure him. He shoves me off him and backs away from me, crawling backward to put as much distance as he can between us.

"Connor..." I start after him, but he holds his hands up, halting me in my tracks.

"You don't understand. I have no control. I can see everything that's happening, but I can't do shit to stop it. He made me rape Mary last night. Fuck, I even defiled you," he rambles on a hiccup, and I drop down on my ass as last night unlocks and comes back to me full-force. Mary's cries of pleasure, the way Connor's hand felt rubbing me through my jeans, all of it.

The entire night plays out like a bad memory as I remember each and every helpless moment we were all forced in. So many emotions fill me at once that I have to close my eyes from the onslaught of them. But, one thing from last night stands out the most to me. Connor's beautiful body as he disappeared inside Mary. My cock twitches and I mentally curse myself for that sick shit.

"He defiled us all. That wasn't you, Connor, that was him," I tell him, trying to ground myself from the reality of the fucked-up situation we're in.

"I can't stop him," he cries out, dropping his head in his hands as his chest heaves for air. I rush over and wrap my arms around him, not caring one bit about how he tries to fight me off of him.

Eventually, he gives up and wraps his arms around me, clinging to me like a lifeline while he dry heaves, burying his head in my chest and using me as his anchor. I hold him tight, wanting so badly to tell him it's going to be okay, but I would never lie to him. We are knee-deep in a shit pool right now with no ladder to climb out of it.

"I got you. I won't let him do this shit again, okay? I will restrain you if I have to." Making such a promise to him breaks my soul, but it calms him down enough to get his head back on his shoulders.

"I've never had sex before last night. That's not how I envisioned shit going. Rose petals and candles lit maybe, but not that.

Mary's going to fucking hate my guts now. All of you should," he says as I wipe the tears away from his cheeks and place gentle kisses along his jawline. His breath catches, but he doesn't stop me.

"Mary can't hate you. It wasn't you, baby. I could never hate you either. Pretty sure I'm just as fucked for you as I am for her." I need to give him a part of me to keep him strong right now until we can figure this out. He turns his face toward me and glances down at my lips as I peek my tongue out to lick away a stray tear. He comes forward and slams his mouth against mine, taking what he wants, and I let him. He had no power or control last night, so I damn sure will give it back any way I can. "Let me show you how it's supposed to be," I beg him when I pull away. Losing your virginity shouldn't go like it did with him. When he nods a little, I lay him down on the dust-covered floor before crawling up his body and nibbling his ear. "I won't take you all the way. Need lube for that. But I will make you feel good," I reassure him, and he releases a sigh as I start trailing kisses down his neck and run my hand underneath his shirt, letting out a groan at the textured abs I feel. He's fit and hard compared to Mary's softness.

When I reach down and pop the button of his jeans, he sucks in a breath as he becomes lost in the haze of lust. Picking his hips up a bit to help me, I shimmy his pants down below his ass as his hard cock springs out and slaps against his shirt.

I give him no warning or time before I lean down and suck him to the back of my throat. Not having a gag reflex comes in handy. He releases a long, drawn-out groan as his hands come down and grips my hair to hold on for the ride. I flatten my tongue on the underside of his length and drag my mouth back to his tip. That's when he spares a simple glance down at me to see what I'm doing to him. He tastes like male and need as I watch the sparks ignite in his eyes. I toy with him for a second and jiggle my tongue over his head drawing a groan from his chest.

Fuck, if his face isn't a vision. Mouth parted, cheeks flushed, and sweat already gathering by the droplets on his forehead. He drops his head back to the floor with a thump and I chuckle a little before descending on him again and driving him out of his mind. He starts to lift his hips to fuck my mouth from below, but I stop him right when I know he's on the edge of coming undone.

I pull off him with a pop and sit back on my knees, reaching for my own jeans and pulling them down my ass enough to get my own cock out.

"Holy fuck, you're pierced!?!" he says, examining my Jacob's ladder with nothing but need in his eyes.

"Yeah. I lost a bet after I graduated from high school, and this was the result. No regrets either because it feels amazing, especially for the one receiving." I grin wickedly at him as he flushes. I crook my finger, beckoning him closer. He gets to his knees and shuffles toward me awkwardly with his pants hanging just below his ass. I whip my shirt off over my head and he follows my actions with his own.

I grab him by the back of his neck and bring him flush against me before fitting his mouth on mine once more. When his cock rubs against mine, I fist us both with my free hand and start to massage our cocks together, or as much of them as I can grip. Connor's no small man and neither am I, so it takes a second for me to find the right angle to jack us together.

He doesn't notice or seem to care as he groans and fucks my mouth with his tongue. He's devouring me like a man that's starving, but honestly, I'm doing the same. His hands are touching me everywhere they can like he's been denied touch for too long.

I feel the signs of my approaching orgasm as we kneel in front of each other chest to chest in a haunted asylum and a goddamn ghost possessing his body. What a hell of a first memory to have with each other.

Connor grips my hips hard as his length starts to pulse in my grip and his cum paints us both. I'm not far behind him, marking him just as he did me as our chests heave for air.

He pulls away from me, looking sated and satisfied, and smiling with a giddy look in his eyes.

"Nick, I...," he starts to say, but his face quickly turns ashen, and his eyes look troubled.

"What is it, baby? Tell me," I demand, reaching for him to hold him to me, but he shakes his head, backing away and redressing himself quickly, not caring one bit about the mess of our releases.

"He's back. He's waking up. I'm going to find somewhere to lock myself in. You have to get the others and get the fuck out of here." He jumps to his feet quickly and takes off as I'm left shouting his name with my pants still hanging off my ass.

After I managed to get cleaned up and redressed myself, I tucked Connor's shirt into my back pocket and took off looking for him. Even Jane disappeared with no trace of where she went before Connor and I started fooling around. While I search in vain, I find myself right back where we first started. The smell of decay and sex lingering in the air makes me want to scream and lose my mind.

James has been blowing up my phone since I followed Connor over here, and no matter how much I try to reassure him I'm fine, the overbearing bastard is demanding a face-to-face chat, but I'm not ready to admit defeat and leave Connor behind just yet.

When I can't take any more of the constant pinging of my phone, I whip it out and call him via face chat.

"What!?!" I scream, letting him know now isn't the greatest time. My emotions are getting the best of me, but this place seems to be drawing it out and feeding on my energy.

"Where the fuck are you? I've been texting you for hours, but you've barely told me anything, Nick. Where's Connor?" James demands, but a frigid chill runs up my spine as the room temperature seems to drop several degrees.

"Hold up. Something's happening right now," I whisper and motion for him to screen record this as Mary appears over his shoulder, looking like she has the flu. I'm concerned as fuck about her, but I can't lose my head right now, because something tells me I'm about to have some activity from beyond the grave.

James nods, flicks at his screen, and starts recording as a child-like giggle fills the surrounding room. The sound is hollow and echoes like it's bouncing off the walls in several directions, which puts me on edge. I don't care who you are, nothing and I do mean *nothing*, is more terrifying than a ghost kid giggle.

Squeaking draws my attention to the left as I move my phone to show a tricycle slowly starting to move on its own, the pedals turning and the handlebars shifting slightly as it moves and comes closer to me. I don't move or hardly breathe as the energy in the room multiplies tenfold. It feels like I'm surrounded, yet there's nothing here at all other than the forgotten remains of this place.

"We're seeing some shadows, Nick. They're small, so you are definitely having child spirits coming through right now," Mary whispers gently, even as she looks close to puking. Of course, the camera is picking up stuff the naked eye can't see.

The bike stops moving suddenly and the child-like giggles stop. Even as hot as it is here, the room keeps dropping in temperature, to the point I can see my breath puff out in front of me.

The hairs on the back of my neck stand on end as I hear claws scratch the floor behind me. I slowly turn the camera around and lift it slightly to point over my shoulder as my chest thumps violently with the trashing of my heartbeat. I hear James and Mary suck in sharp breaths, letting me know whatever the fuck is behind me isn't something I'm going to like.

"Don't. Move. Nick," my big brother whispers, punctuating each word. I want to reply, 'No shit, dumbasses,' but the only mantra flowing through my head right now is, 'Please, don't eat me. Please, don't eat me.'

I feel a puff of icy breath hit the back of my neck and try so violently not to flinch. My butthole is puckered, and I have a heavy sense that I'm in quite the pickle here. When another puff of cold air skitters along my shoulders, I squeeze my eyes closed and start praying silently that if this thing does eat me; it kills me in one bite. Phone forgotten completely, I focus on remaining as still as I can. I don't want to feel myself being chomped on. Somehow, I know a hit is coming and tense up for the inevitable. I feel the thing reach out, but before it makes contact with me, a dodgeball comes flying across the room and right over my shoulder.

The temperature seems to increase now, and I open my eyes to see a little boy in front of me. His little frame flickers as he stands and observes me. I slowly bring the phone down and turn it back around, hoping that James and Mary are capturing this incorporeal entity.

"Hi, I'm Nick," I whisper, hoping I don't scare him off. I'm still stiff as shit from the boogeyman picking over my body like a lunch menu.

"You're a dumbass, Nick," the little kid replies, squinting at me like I might be in the slow department and I'm stunned stupid for a second.

"The fuck?" I rear back with my lip arched in a confused state.

"I said, you are a dumbass, Nick," the kid replies again, letting out a chuckle over my expression.

"And why is that?" I ask curiously and force myself to relax at this little dude's easy nature.

"Because you smell like butt farts and looked like you were about to cry like a sissy. You a sissy, mister?" the kid questions me. Tilting his head slightly like he's studying me.

"Uh, no. I'm not a sissy, you shit. Something was about to eat me," I reply, trying to explain my reaction to the creature that was just behind me. I go from relaxed to defensive in two seconds flat. How the hell am I getting rimmed by a ghost kid right now?

"George? He don't eat folks. He likes dolls. Anyone that ever comes here always leaves him a doll. We ain't had visitors in a long time so he was just excited is all," the kid says with a rich, southern accent before wiping at his nose with his arm. He looks sad but mischievous at the same time. His clothes look like they date back to the forties, maybe fifties. A white worn shirt and a pair of faded overalls paired with shoes that look two sizes too small.

"What's your name, kid?" I assess him more, trying to remember he's dead. Something about this kid is drawing my protective side out and I don't know why.

"Billy. Billy Simons," he answers and starts to fidget around like he's in trouble. My guess is the last time he was questioned he ended up dead so I can understand his sudden distress.

It's blowing my mind to be having a conversation with a spirit right now like this. We've never had this kind of experience before with an almost incorporeal form that is very lucid. I take a quick glance at my phone and notice the screen is black like it cut off during my encounter with George.

"You should probably get gone before he comes back though. I saw you come in with *him* a while ago. You need to be careful around him," the kid says, giving me a hard look like he's a scolding parent.

"Who? Connor?" I ask, but the look in the kid's eyes tells me I didn't have to ask. He glances over his shoulder and gasps before disappearing into thin air. I start to run toward him, but I tilt over my feet and slam against the wooden floor face first. Groaning, I roll over and let go of my phone to bring my hands up to check for damage. When I'm sure I didn't just shatter my nose, I sit up and look down at my pitter-patters to see my shoelaces tied together.

I hear what must be Billy laughing before it fades away, and I roll my eyes at his shenanigans. Redoing my shoelaces correctly, I brush off the dust, grab my phone, and stand once more. I smash my finger on my phone screen to reconnect to James again. I wish like hell I could have gotten some of this Billy footage.

I take one last look around before heading out to go find James and Mary with a heavy heart. I've got to figure out how to save Connor.

FIVE

James

Nick found our stash of granola bars and protein bars, and that was our lunch. My stomach still growls for more, but we need to conserve what we have if we are trapped in here for the foreseeable future.

"Did you call the owner again?" Nick asks. "Did you tell him we'll sue his fucking balls off? I'll leave them here for Billy to play with."

"I can't believe we captured the kid on video," I breathe out. "I tried calling the asshole over twenty times today already, but the calls keep cutting out. My phone and Mary's won't do outbound calls. We can call each other though."

"There's something fucked-up here, and it has everything to do with Conroy," Mary whispers from her cot.

She's been laying there, despondent since we came out of the bathroom. I forced her to eat a granola bar and have a bottle of warm water, but she could barely get that down.

"Do you think he's the one who has us trapped in here?" I ask her as Nick chews noisily on his protein bar.

"Yes, no doubt. He won't let us leave without him."

"There's no way we're leaving Connor here. We need to find him, then we need to somehow get that thing out of him."

"I can't be here another night," Mary says, choking on a sob.

"It's too much."

"We won't let that happen to you again—"

She cuts me off, eyeballing me with daggers in her eyes. "Could you stop it last night? When he had you strapped to your cot as if you were a patient?"

"He won't do it a second time," Nick promises as he goes to sit beside her on the narrow bed. Her arm winds around his waist, and my first instinct is to want to rip him away from her. I should be the one consoling her.

I've been wanting to, but too afraid of making her feel worse. She was defiled, *raped*, and I didn't know if she'd want my touch. It's no secret the life she endured as a child. We were all children, but we did try to save her many times. It wasn't until we turned sixteen that she finally went to the police and her uncle was arrested. Her cousins hate her for it, and any family she had left turned their backs on her. Everyone but the three of us.

"We stay awake tonight," I growl out, my emotions still running high. "If I can't get that door open."

"While you do that, I'm going to find Connor." Nick tries to stand, but Mary's arm tightens around him.

"Be careful, Nick," she murmurs. "When that thing is inside of him, he's not Connor."

"He's always Connor, Mary." Nick runs his fingers through her hair. "He's in there still, trying to fight his way out. We can't give up on him."

Nick continues to stroke her hair, reassuring her we're here, and soon enough, she falls asleep.

"She needs to rest," I mutter. "I'm so worried about her."

"She's the strongest person I know," Nick says in a rare moment of vulnerability. He gently eases her back onto the cot. "If she's this messed up, then we need to get out of here and soon."

"I need to work on that fucking door," I tell him as I grab up my tool bag again.

"I'll go find Connor." The worried look on his face only confirms what I've suspected for so long. Nick and Connor are in love.

74

When we were kids, there were signs, lingering touches and longing looks, but I chalked it up to the confusion of adolescence. Now I see it differently, and even though last night is still much of a blur for me, I do remember what happened between the two of them.

Maybe it was because their lust overpowered whatever cold energy Conroy was projecting.

I don't know how this dynamic will work between the four of us. I want Mary, and always have, but I know the other two do as well. Yet, now I see they want each other too. Is this something they will give up Mary for? Will they be together, leaving me to have my one true love for myself?

It's the only scenario I see that works smoothly, but nothing about us is smooth. Maybe, somehow, we'll all have Mary, and they'll still have each other. Would that even work?

I try everything on the door, and out of all of us, I'm the strongest, but there's some sort of barrier around it and the windows too. My hammer rushes toward the door, but an inch from its surface, it's cushioned by something, and my blows don't connect.

It's taking all of my energy, and yet, there isn't one fucking dent in the wood.

Sweat courses down my face, and my chest heaves with each of my labored breaths, all the while my stomach groans for food.

"Fuck," I snap, as I grab my phone back out of my pocket. I dial the landlord's number again, only to hear a crackling, white noise coming from the speaker.

My arms drop to my sides, and my chin hits my chest in defeat. How can I be the leader when I can't even get this fucking door open?

"James?"

I turn at the sound of Mary's tired voice, finding her standing behind me. She looks exhausted still, but the sight of her chewing into another granola bar has my spirits soaring.

"Sorry, did I wake you up?"

She steps into me, her arms wrapping around my waist, and her face pressing into my chest.

"You're working so hard to get us out of here," she whispers. "Thank you."

She somehow is always so attuned to my emotions, and when I slip into the pool of deprecation, she manages to pull me out.

I drag her in closer, feeling her soft body molding to my hardened one, and without thought, a moan slips from my mouth. She feels like she was made to fit every sharp edge of my body. Her head tips up, her chin resting against my chest, and without further thought, I lean down and press my mouth to hers.

Her hands slip up under my shirt at my back, her granola bar hitting the floor at our feet, and her fingers splaying out along my skin. I part her lips with my tongue, and when she gasps, I invade her hot mouth, filling it eagerly. My cock thickens against her, and when I grind into her, I feel her stiffen.

Shame, hot and all-consuming scorch over me, and I quickly pull away, stumbling backward into the door.

"Fuck, Mary, I'm so sorry." My body trembles as I stare at her in shock.

This is our first actual kiss, and I did it inside a haunted asylum after she's been brutally raped, twice. What the fuck is wrong with me?

Her head shakes as her fingers shakily run over her lips. Then, to my shock, she's coming forward, and pulling me back into her, wrapping me up in a hug. I gather her to me, inhaling her sweet scent.

"You can't know how much I needed that," she mumbles. "To feel desired and wanted after what happened last night."

"I will always want you, Mary," I confess, because it's now or never. "There's no one else for me, and what happened last night is not your fault."

She rises on her tiptoes and presses her mouth to mine, her soft, breathy moan making it hard to hold myself together.

"I want you too, James. I didn't want our first moment to belong to this place either, but you may have just saved me."

She's looking at me like I'm her hero when all I'm feeling is weak. I can't get us out of here, and the thought of putting her through another night tears me apart.

"Go on back and lie down." I kiss her cheek and let go of her. "I'm going to keep at this door."

The sun is beginning to set when Nick reappears, his face looking sad and scared.

"No luck?" I ask him.

He shakes his head and heads to the bathroom, his shoulders hunched forward. This fucking place is chipping at us bit by bit, and for the first time since we arrived, I have an insight into exactly how every patient felt as they were trapped inside these walls.

I finally give up on the door and head back to the cots, knowing I'm going to have to face Mary and tell her we're still trapped. I find her sitting and watching the receptionist's desk with steady rapture.

"Mary?"

"I think I saw her last night," Mary murmurs, her head tipping in skepticism. "The secretary."

"Really?" The hairs begin to rise along my arms at the sound of her faraway voice.

"I think she's the one who let us in yesterday. I have a feeling she's watching us and wants us in here," she continues. "Maybe if I talk to her, she'll help us get out."

"Wait," I say, sitting on the bed next to her. "Am I the only one who hasn't seen a ghost here? You've seen the secretary, Nick, a little kid, and Connor…"

"She was holding her head." I watch as her eyes widen and her throat works on a swallow. "Conroy really chopped her head off."

"How do you think she can help us out of here?"

She gets up from her cot and grabs my hand, pulling me

77

towards the large desk. "I checked this out earlier while you were busy with the door." She opens the top drawer and pulls out a piece of paper. It's old and yellowing, but there, written in perfect cursive at the top, it says, 'The Duties of Belgrove's Secretary.'

"Look what that first duty says," she whispers.

"Ensure the doors stay locked, and don't let anyone out without a visitor's pass," I read. "We need to find passes."

I begin to yank open drawers when Mary's hand lands on my arm. "There aren't any here, I checked already," she says. "But maybe they were kept somewhere else"

"It's a great idea," I mutter as I grab the flashlight. "The sun's gone down, and I think we need to search for them now."

"Search for what?" Nick asks as he comes out of the bathroom.

"Visitor passes." I wave him off. "I'll explain as we go. Did you, by chance, see a director's office, or an office where the head physician would be while you were going around this place?"

Nick's head tips upward as he looks up at the top of the stairs. "Hey, buddy." He waves and then hits my arm, his eyes staying focused on the top of the stairs. "Billy's here. Can you see him?"

Mary and I both scan the stairs and the second floor, but we don't find anything out of place. "No…" I trail off and shake my head.

"He says he can take us to the mean doctor's office. He says it's on the second floor." Nick rushes forward. "Hey, little buddy, have you seen my friend, Connor?" he asks as he gets to the top and looks down at the floor at his feet.

"This is so weird," I murmur.

"He's not my boyfriend!" Nick scoffs, his hands landing on his hips.

My eyes meet Mary's and her mouth tips slightly with a small smile. "I wonder what we missed. Do you think they finally…?"

"Maybe. Trauma brings out different things in different people."

"It's been something growing between them for a while. I

think it was about to make its appearance whether we were here or not," Mary replies with a hum as we start up the stairs.

"The children's ward is that way." Nick points to the right. "Just past the breezeway, but Billy says the director's office and file rooms are that way." He points to the left.

The corridor is dark, the cobwebs heavy along the corners of the ceiling. The darkness doesn't hold the same sinister vibe as the basement, but the energy is still ominous.

Nick rushes ahead with his little, invisible friend while Mary slips her hand into mine, sending arcs of electricity up my arm. My fingers squeeze around her small ones, and contentment settles in my chest.

Finally.

Mary

Yesterday, when we stood outside the front doors, attempting to force our way into this hell, I remember hearing a voice. *Mary, are you quite contrary?* She sounded whimsical, her lilting voice caressing my ears.

I truly believe the secretary was the one to let us through the doors, and the only reason she's not letting us out is because we haven't proved we're not patients. To her, we may be newly admitted, and waiting for treatment. She's just doing her job after all.

"The second floor isn't as bad as the basement," I murmur, and warmth falls over me as James squeezes my hand again.

"Because the moonlight is making its way in through the broken windows. If there weren't any bars, I would attempt to climb out of one." His flashlight swoops along the wide corridor, highlighting the webs and crumbling walls.

"The moisture is ruining this place. They should just rip it down."

The rooms on either side of the hallway are sealed with enormous steel doors, a single window, and one slot decorating their surfaces. This is where the adults stayed, minus Conroy. The ones people believed were beyond saving because they loved the same sex, or their families didn't have the time or patience to deal with mental illnesses. It breaks my heart because they didn't have the medications we do now, and some of these people weren't crazy. They just needed a little help and a good support system. Electroshock wasn't the answer though.

"Over here, guys!" Nick calls out. "I found the office."

We hurry to the room he just disappeared into, and rush in behind him. There's a large, oak desk, and a nameplate still sitting precariously on the edge. *Dr. Morris.*

"Billy says Dr. Morris was a cunt." Nick snorts as he moves to the filing cabinet.

"What's Billy's story?" I ask. "Why was he here?"

The chair on the other side of the desk creaks and moves as if someone is sitting in it, but to my eye it's empty. Nick looks that way, and that's when I know he can really see Billy. I can tell by the way his eyes rove over the chair as if listening and paying attention to something someone is saying.

"Billy liked to try on his mom's clothes sometimes, and she caught him," Nick repeats Billy's story to us. "She sent him here to make sure he didn't grow up to become homosexual."

My hand clasps over my mouth because poor Billy never made it out of here alive. My eyes burn with the onslaught of tears and my throat swells with emotion. It never fails to astonish me how hard some children's lives are, despite having a horrific one myself.

"What happened to you?" James asks, as if reading my mind.

We wait while Nick listens to the boy in the chair, his eyes growing sad. "He was given electroshock therapy, a specialty of Dr. Morris' here. Something went wrong and Billy says he never made it out of the basement alive again."

"I wish we thought to stream this," James mumbles.

"Not everything is meant to be publicized," Nick chastises. "Billy's story isn't ours to tell."

"He's right," I agree.

"Billy says a lot of bodies are buried out back in Bedlams Playground. That all the souls roam these hallways, waiting for their loved ones to take them home. The children are the worst because he says they can't tell that they're dead."

"Oh, no," I moan. "That's terrible."

"Wait, Billy! Who's here?" Nick calls out as the chair begins to spin, as if someone had jumped out of it. "He disappeared."

A low growl slips into the room, followed by a dark chuckle. "I think I know why," James mutters as I look over my shoulder, finding Connor leaning against the doorframe.

"Where the fuck have you been?" Nick bellows.

"You don't own me," Conroy snaps. "I may be in your lover's body, but I'm not your lover. If you try any of that gay shit with me, I'll snap your fucking neck."

Conroy steps into the room, using the boy I love's body to terrorize us. The door slams shut behind him as James turns on a growl, running to attack the phantom menace. With one flick of his wrist, James is propelled to the other side of the room, his large body hitting the plaster with a loud *crack*.

"James!" I scream as I run toward him.

"Oh, no, little girl." Conroy snaps his fingers, the sound attacking my eardrums. "You stay right there." One second, I am rushing towards James, and then suddenly, I can't move a muscle.

"Don't you touch her!" Nick screams, but when I turn to look at him, I can see he's frozen as well.

"This isn't where I thought we'd have round two of our fun, but it'll do." Conroy's arm swipes through the air, and all the files and dust sitting on the desk are wiped to the floor. "Up you go, little one." He gives me an eerie smile as some kind of force moves me to the desk.

"No!" Nick exclaims as James groans from the corner. "Don't hurt her!"

"I saw you getting cozy earlier with the big brother. That kiss was pleasant." Conroy grabs Connor's hardening dick in his hand while speaking to Mary. "Even your boy inside here"—he points to his temple—"liked it too."

81

"Stay away from her," Nick groans out as he tries to break the bonds holding him.

"Oh, I'm not going to have fun with her... this time." Conroy focuses on me as Connor's hands wrap around my waist, lifting me to sit on the desk. "Connor had his fun today." Conroy points to the dried fluid staining his shirt. "Nick has some to match," he says with a wink.

"I don't care," I whisper. "Get your hands off me."

My body begins to tremble as fear slowly seeps back in. I don't want him inside of me again. I don't want to be ashamed of the way my body enjoys it.

"It seems James is the only one who hasn't had his fun lately. That's not fair," Conroy tuts. "Come on over, big man."

James slowly rises to his feet but stays rooted to the corner, his hands forming into fists and his eyes shooting rage towards Conroy.

"Oh, he's angry." Connor leans forward, his mouth touching my ear. "It makes me so hot." His hand moves into James' track pants, and I'm unable to stop him as his cold fingers run along my slit. "She's soaked."

A whimper flies from my lips as a finger slips inside of me as my body remains frozen in place on the desk. My fingers curl through the dust lining the wood surface as my knees sty locked around the edge. Nick howls at the top of his lungs, but James rushes forward, shoving Connor out of the way.

"She's aching, dripping wet," Conroy taunts as he stumbles backward. "If you don't take care of her, I will."

My sweater begins to move over my head, and I can't seem to stop my arms from rising, aiding in its removal.

"Stop!" James bellows. "She's been through enough."

"Has she?" Conroy snickers. "Ask her how badly she wants you to fuck her right now." Nick has grown quiet, his face a bright red and his eyes downcast as he tries not to stare at my naked chest, I would assume out of respect, but all it does is makes my pussy clench in anticipation. Both brothers are here, and Connor is also somewhere inside his body, watching as everything is happening. I can feel my arousal on my thighs. Why am I like this? "Take her pants off, James, see for yourself."

"It's okay," I try to soothe him. "I'd rather it be you."

James pulls my pants off as Nick curses, the front of his pants tightening with his hardening cock. As soon as my bare ass hits the desk, I groan with an all-consuming need. If I focus on James and Nick, I'll be able to get through this.

"Spread her thighs," Conroy demands. "Nick, get a closer look."

Nick is forced closer to us by Conroy, his jaw tight and his eyes averted from me. I can't say it doesn't hurt. I want him to want to look at me.

I fall back to my elbows as James spreads my thighs, my eyes staying firmly on Nick, who's staring at the wall over my head.

"Taste her," Conroy instructs, his voice dropping a few octaves. "Suck on that wet pussy. Fuck, I can see her glistening from here."

When James' mouth lands on me with a groan, I moan so loudly that Nick's eyes finally meet mine. They grow hooded as he sees the pleasure coating my features, and then he allows himself to watch his brother eating my pussy with relish. James' tongue is sure and strong, stroking over my clit with firm swipes.

"Nick is so hard, I can see his cock jerking behind that zipper," Conroy says with a chuckle. "Go on, little girl, free him from his confines."

Nick's eyes are still watching James as he devours me, and I lean up on trembling arms, reaching for the button on Nick's pants. I quickly free him, and his cock springs forward, snatching a gasp from my mouth. James pops his head up and follows my line of sight to his brother's heavily pierced cock.

"Oh my god," I moan the words as I think about him pushing it into me.

"James, she's close," Conroy interrupts. "Get your pants off and your dick inside of her now."

James removes his shirt and pants, both hitting the floor, and then he climbs over me, his eyes begging me for permission even though we both know we don't have a choice.

"It's okay," I comfort him. "I want this."

Not a second passes by after I say the words and he's pushing inside of me as Nick groans, the sound making my pussy clench around James' length.

Nick

All I can do right now is clench my fists at my sides and pray this happens quickly. None of us has control, just like Connor said. Conroy can contort us to his will, and there isn't a thing we can do to stop it.

Watching James fuck Mary right in front of me is doing some shit to my head. My cock leaks precum at the moans coming out of her and the steady thrusts James does in a perfect rhythm that seems to be driving her wild. This isn't supposed to happen like this. It's wrong.

James looks back at me from his spot on the desk and from the look in his eyes, he just knows I'm about to lose my fucking shit. I'm trembling and vibrating with the need to scream and rage over this.

"Stay with me, little brother. I'm right here," James says as he keeps thrusting into Mary. I can see the past storming in his eyes, but instead of us trying to save Mary from the hell she was in, it's us doing it to her.

Tears start to form in my eyes, and James quickly shifts Mary until her face is level with my cock. James reaches out, gripping my hard length and starts to stroke. I gasp as he runs his thumb along my piercings, like he's studying them to see what feels good. I'm frozen and unable to move at all. While I want to rip myself out of his hand, my body wants it.

"Stay with me, little brother. I'm right here," he says again, and I find myself looking down at Mary as her eyes stay locked on where my big brother is jerking me off right in her face.

"This is wrong and so fucked up," I grit out even as pleasure starts coursing its way through me.

The dark, cackling laugh lets me know Conroy is enjoying my

distress far too fucking much, and it's that very thought that helps form a plan in my head. If I can keep Conroy's attention on me, he will leave Mary and James the fuck alone. I can take it for them.

"I'm going to be sick," I breathe out, trying to get Conroy to play into my hands. James increases his speed and grip on me, causing me to hiss as the ecstasy works its way up my spine. Mary's tongue peeks out, licking at my tip, and she moans as my flavor hits her. My jaw drops at the innocent act, and I'm pretty sure she isn't aware of what she just did. James looks equally shocked, but he picks up his thrusts and jacks me to the beat of them. I hear Conroy groan, but I can't look at him right now. I know damn well I'll see Connor pleasuring himself and not Conroy molesting him.

A groan creeps out of my throat, and James grips me tightly, making sure I'm aware he heard me. "You can stop," I whisper to him, but a look of determination fills his eyes as he starts to bring Mary and me to the brink of an orgasm.

Mary licks at me again and the softness of her tongue has me bending and gripping the desk tightly for balance.

"You really can't do that again, babe. I will blow my load all over your face and I'm trying to behave right now." I try to get her to understand that I'm not a willing participant in this. Now I fully understand why Connor was out of his mind when we were together. This kind of trauma never heals. It's going to linger with me forever. I'm finally getting to be with the two people I want most in life but the price we are paying for it is more scars on our souls than happy memories being made.

"It's okay, Nick. I want you just as much as them. Use my mouth and focus on me," she replies, and I can feel myself jerk in James' hold. I look up at him and he gives me a devilish grin. Fuck it. I tried to be a gentleman.

James lets go of me as I grip myself and tease Mary's lips. She licks at my piercings as I guide myself into her warm, wet mouth, almost to the back of her throat. I'm not trying to be an asshole and gag her, but when she sucks at me, I thrust a little, causing her to choke.

She reaches out and grips my hips and starts to control the thrusts herself, moaning and writhing under James. She's close and so are we.

James' hand comes up to grab my shoulder to balance himself as Mary lets out a muffled scream around my cock. They both let go and I'm not far behind as my length pulses with my release and coats Mary's tongue.

The sexiest sight I've ever seen is her sucking on me to clean me up after swallowing most of my cum. James watches her with rapt fascination before he pulls free of her and grips her legs, opening her to his eyes.

I lean over and watch as his cum trickles from her perfect, pink pussy and groan slightly at the erotic view. I know my brother well. It's not that we have a breeding kink or anything, but that sight right there is like marking what we know is ours.

A slow clap brings us back to the situation at hand and we turn to face Conroy. He looks giddy as shit and I want to scream.

"You're welcome. Honestly, if you all weren't such prudes, imagine the fun we could have," he says, chuckling slightly.

"Forcing yourself on others isn't fun, Conroy. It's fucking sick," I snarl because I'm over this motherfucker.

"Temper, temper, little brother," Conroy replies, mocking James and me. James rolls off the desk and helps Mary down. I pull her into me, wrapping my arms tightly around her as James stands in front of us to block Conroy's view.

"You all really spoil the mood. I'm going to find fun elsewhere." We watch as he walks out of the room, whistling as he goes in that same haunting tune as before. I don't miss the cum spot left on the floor where he was standing either.

The negative energy seems to leave the room with him, and we all breathe a little in relief. James starts to grab our clothes, and I'm startled by Billy suddenly returning and sitting in the desk chair. Jane reappears as well, darting into the room with her tail wagging happily like she's just happy to be here right now. She plops her ass down and scratches behind her ear before looking us all over with her tongue hanging out her mouth.

"Why are you guys naked?" he asks innocently, and the awkwardness starts to settle inside me hard. How am I supposed to explain sex to a ghost kid? I cover my dick with my hands trying to shield my decorated man member from him. It's one thing to educate

86

him on the birds and the bees. Explaining my piercings is a whole other monster.

"Uh…" I try to think of something, but my brain blanks.

"Billy's here, isn't he?" Mary asks, turning into me and trying to use my body to shield as much of hers as possible. I let my dick go and hold my hands in front of her luscious ass cheeks, very tempted to squeeze them, but remembering Billy's in the room so I have to behave myself.

"Give us like five minutes my man. Um, I don't know how much of the when a man and a woman love each other very much talk you've had, but I am not about to explain this shi..stuff to you," I tell Billy, tripping over my curse and trying to be respectful of his tender age.

James finds her shirt and gets it over her head. We all start getting dressed as Billy waits and watches us patiently. For a little dude, he has no shame in studying us like he's completely unbothered by it. A horrible thought enters my mind that makes me think he was subjected to some unimaginable shit in this damn place.

"I think I have a patient that can help you out," he finally says as I get my pants buttoned up.

"If that patient's anything like Conroy, no fucking thank you," I snap back and wince because while we only had to deal with the sick fuck for two days, Billy and the others have had to deal with him in life, and we unleashed this hell on them, even after their deaths when they should be resting and at peace.

"Nope. This chick got the buzz like me, but she did this whole smile and cursed their souls thing before she expired. I watched the whole thing," Billy rambles, reminiscing on his time here. He looks thoughtful about it as he taps his chin recounting the ordeal. The fact he's unbothered by a horrendous event like that makes me feel sick on his behalf. This kid is tough and courageous.

"What's he saying?" Mary asks, holding onto my arm as James hugs her from behind and nuzzles her neck. "Does he know where the passes are?"

"Visitor passes? Yeah, right here in the desk. But you should know Mary isn't going to let y'all leave. She always did her duty first," Billy replies, and I'm confused as fuck.

"Mary?" I ask and hold up a finger to Mary's lips to shush her.

"Yeah. The secretary. I need to help you find that other patient first though," Billy remarks, hopping up from the desk and reaching towards the drawer of the desk. His hand passes through it but a moment later it slides open as if air alone guided it. "Mary won't let you leave with your friend. She knows Conroy is inside of him."

"I'll come with you. If this patient can help with the Conroy thing, then I'm in," I tell him, turning slightly to give Mary a kiss on her head and clamping down on James' shoulders.

"You watch her closely, big bro. I'll be back later," I tell him. I give Mary one last lingering look to make sure she isn't seeing me in a negative way after what we just did. While I don't regret it, I hate the way it transpired. She gives me a soft smile that tugs at my heart and lets me know we're going to be okay. Turning back towards the door, I let out a breath and follow Billy.

Fuck me. Rule number one of any horror movie ever, never say what I just did.

Bedlam's Playground

SIX
Mary

"The secretary's name was Mary, like me."

"And you're the only one who's seen her," James says as he gently guides me out of the door. He's just fucked me to within an inch of my life, and now he's treating me like I'm made of glass.

"Listen." I turn on him and nearly laugh when the largest man in our group steps back with apprehension. "What we did in there wasn't how I saw our first time going, but I don't regret it. I'm not hurt. I wanted you, and I enjoyed it. Do you understand me?"

His eyes darken, and suddenly, he closes the space between us, his hands wrapping around my face. "I love you, Mary Young."

"I love you too, James Harrison."

Connor and the Harrison boys have always owned my heart. It's just taken me a long time to admit it. Now that it's out there, I don't want to be treated like I'm damaged or fragile. I'm neither of those things.

I am strong and I'm a survivor. Nothing short of a fucking soldier.

His mouth seals over mine in a sweet kiss, one that makes my toes curl inside of my shoes. I'm finally ready to have a relationship with them, and I say *them* because I couldn't imagine not being with each of them. Connor, Nick, and James all own my heart equally. People already think we're having one big orgy every night, so why not make it a reality?

I would have to make it crystal clear to Nick and Connor that I don't mind their relationship either. In fact, I encourage it. Nothing about the four of us is normal, and I am done fighting it.

"As sweet as this is," a sweet voice interrupts us, "I think there are more pressing issues besides your lips."

I let out a scream, the piercing sound echoing around our heads and bouncing off of the decrepit walls. "What the hell?" I turn to find a woman in a pink pair of scrubs, but it's not the sight of the secretary's ghost that throws me off. It's the fact that her neck is a bloody stump where her head should be, and the head itself is tucked into the crook of her arm like a fucking football.

"What is it?" James' arm wraps around my waist as his body tenses.

"Mary," I whisper.

"Yes, that's me," she says, her shoulders tipping forward and that stump moving as if in a nod. "And it's you. Now that we have formalities out of the way, are you looking to escape my facility?"

"Not escape." I shake my head. "To leave, we are guests."

"Visitors?" That creepy head of hers tilts in her arms and I choke back a gasp.

"Yes." I reach behind me to grab the passes out of James' hands and show them to her. "Here are four visitor passes."

"Four?" Her lips turn down slightly as she looks at the passes in my hand. "There are only three of you here who are new. I have not seen a fourth."

"Our friend, Connor, is here as a visitor as well but something has happened to him. We need to leave."

"Conroy is inside of Connor, and if I know that psycho as well as I think I do—he took my head after all—then he's never leaving his body, and I cannot let him leave this place. I can sense him festering inside your friend, slowly draining everything that was once Connor, and taking over as Conroy. If he is allowed to, he will leave this place and continue the massacre he started all those years ago."

"What is she saying?" James whispers in my ear.

"She won't let Connor leave until Conroy leaves his body."

"It makes sense," James mutters. "I don't want Conroy leaving with us either. I'm hoping Billy pulls through and we find the other patient to help."

"This friend of yours is talking about the witch," Mary sneers at us. "She's a fraud. Batshit crazy, hence why she was in this place. Did you know she loved to sacrifice things? Cats, rabbits, ex-husbands."

"Shit," I curse with a frustrated moan.

"What?" James asks.

"That patient may not be a witch. She may just be crazy."

The eyes on the head Mary is holding rolls, the whites of her eyes becoming the most prominent before looking at us once more. "Obviously she's crazy. She was here at Belgrove."

"We may never leave." I sniff as I speak the words, my heart completely shattering at the thought of being stuck here forever.

"No." James turns me around to look into my eyes. "Don't think like that. They used to think being gay was a mental illness. Logically witchcraft would be too."

He's right, of course he's right. I feel like my logical mind was left outside those large entrance doors the moment we stepped into this place.

"If we remove Conroy from our friend," I question as I turn back around to meet Mary's head, "will you let us out of here?"

"You bet." She sounds sarcastic and snarky, much like my normal self. She doesn't believe for a second that we'll save Connor. "Would you two like some coffee? We have a great visitor's area."

"I think Mary may also be a bit deranged," I whisper as the ghost leads us back downstairs.

"She had her head chopped off, Mary," James tsks. "With a fucking ax."

We reach the bottom of the stairs as Mary's muted form glides toward the single bathroom and then makes a right. "You will also clean up this mess you made," she chastises us. "I will not allow your weird machines to run in here. It is prohibited to videotape or record our patients."

"It was her who turned off our generators and made our cell phones stop working," I inform James. "She says it's against Belgrove's rules."

"Makes sense again," James mutters once more. "I wonder what our followers are thinking."

"We can tell them everything as soon as we step out of here."

"It will be hearsay," Mary hums. "I know we cannot control the press. That's what you lot are, right? Reporters and such," she spits out the words with disgust. "But it will always be your word against ours. Trust me, no one cares what happens to the crazy people."

"I think she's floating in the in-between," I tell James as we step into a small room. There's a mint-colored fridge with a matching green table set and six chairs. The dusty counters are also a mint-green, and on the surface, there's an old, empty coffee machine. "She still believes she's a worker here, and she has to protect the patients."

The kitchen is caked in dust and cobwebs, but remarkably clean otherwise.

"Maybe we can help her too," James says as he falls into one of the chairs.

"I will not leave this place," Mary snaps at him as if he can hear him. "I have no family beyond these walls, and these patients need me."

"She doesn't want to leave."

"Fine," he responds with a shrug. "Come here." He pats his leg as Mary scoffs. I can't tell if the noise escapes her stump or her mouth, as she stands stock-still and watches us.

"You aren't even married. This is not very ladylike of you."

I move to sit on James' knee as he runs his fingers through his hair.

"It's a different time now," I try to explain to her. "You've been trapped here for a long time."

"Girls have become free with their bodies?" I swear the head in her hand tips in question, but there's intrigue in her eyes.

"What are you guys talking about?" James asks as he nuzzles my neck, his tongue dipping out to run along the surface of my skin. I can feel him hardening beneath me, and it only heightens my shame. Something I know always seems to get me off.

"She says I'm unladylike." I gasp as he nips at my shoulder, making me press my ass into him.

"Is that right?" I can hear the mischief in his voice as he grabs my hips to grind up into me. "Does she want to see how nasty you can be?"

It's like he knows exactly what I need to get off. "Yes," I keen as I wiggle in his lap. "Tell her how bad I am."

"Are you sure this is what you want?" he whispers in my ear.

"Do your worst."

Degradation, shame, guilt, and self-loathing all contribute to what sexual experience I have, and it's become a necessity to get off. Maybe now that the guys and I have come to some sort of understanding, they can slowly change that for me. But for now, I need to feel filthy.

"Get off my lap and bend over the table. Let's show this *Mary* how you can be a good slut for me."

A moan escapes me at the same time Mary gasps, but she doesn't move from the counter, one hand gripping the edge while the other covers one of the eyes on her head. She's still watching though, her eye wide with shock.

I bend over the table as James pulls down my pants, his ass still seated on the chair. "My cum is dripping out of your filthy cunt," he growls out. "It's still fresh, and yet, here you are begging for more."

He slips a finger inside of me as I place my fist between my teeth, stopping myself from enjoying it. I hate that I need to feel like I'm being used.

"What is he doing to you?" Mary asks, her mouth falling open, that eye still wide on us.

"Tell her what you're doing to me," I tell James.

"This juicy cunt is filled with my cum," he says out loud. "She just finished slurping my brother's cum down her throat while I filled this pussy with mine, and now she wants more." My forehead hits the table as he continues to finger me, the sounds of his cum and my arousal filtering around the room. "You shouldn't be enjoying this," he chastises. "It's wrong, Mary. You're a nasty girl to want this while we're trapped in this place with ghosts."

"I don't want this," I moan, the sound a contrast to the words I'm speaking. "I hate that you make me feel like this."

"Too bad. This is what a slut deserves." The chair scrapes along the floor as he stands, and I can hear the zipper on his jeans lower. "Now, be a good little whore and take all this without a fucking sound. I don't want anyone to hear me fucking you."

He knows everything to say and everything to do, because my pussy is leaking down my thighs with anticipation. The head of his cock presses to my pussy just as Mary begins to mutter a Hail Mary, making me snort into my hand.

"She's praying for us," I tell James as he pushes into me.

"No amount of praying will save your tarnished soul," he flings his words with accuracy. "You're nothing but a soppy cunt for men to fuck." My core clenches around his thick girth, hauling a strangled groan from his throat. His hand claps down on my ass cheek with a loud, resounding *smack*. "Did I say you could enjoy this, slut?"

"Oh god," I whine, pressing my face to the dusty tabletop.

James

I think I like this degradation thing, and even more so because of the way Mary's pussy is dripping and gripping around my length. I know what this does to her, and I understand why she needs it. I continue to plow into her, forcing her narrow hips to hit the edge of the table, making it inch forward with each thrust.

She's a moaning, dripping mess in front of me, and it's heightened further by the audience we have.

My balls are saturated with my cum from earlier and her juices, as they roll downward. I spread open her ass cheeks to find her puckered hole winking up at me. I collect some of our combined release and smear it over the hole, making her jerk forward with a gasp.

"Shut your fucking mouth," I snap at her, my cock jerking in response to my tone. "I can fuck any hole on your body, and because you're a fucking slut, you'll beg me for more. You can cry all you want. I know you want every inch I feed you." I yank my cock out of her, watching as her pussy hole leaks before scooping her juices upward and slathering them all over her asshole, snickering when she clenches. "Doesn't matter what you do." My hand grips her hair, yanking her head upward. "I'm fucking this ass and you will keep your fucking mouth shut." When she doesn't answer, I give her head a shake. "Did you hear me?"

"Yes," she whispers, her words shaky with trepidation.

"Now open up," I demand. She widens her legs as I step between them, gripping her ass cheeks open once more, and pressing my saturated cock to her tight hole. Then, without warning, I roughly begin to thrust into her. Her whimpers of pain are muffled by the hand she has wrapped around her mouth, but it only ramps up my need to fuck her harder. I thrust in again, bottoming out inside her ass, then laugh as a moan escapes her. "Dirty whore." I fuck her ass with abandonment, her hips making the table skirt a little closer to the fridge, and when I feel her begin to clench with her impending release, I pull out of her. "You don't get to come that easily," I tsk. "This is for me, *little girl*." I use the same pet name Conroy did, and the one she told me her uncle once used.

"Please," she whimpers, reaching between her legs to try to bring herself to release as she watches me over her shoulder. "Please, let me come."

I fall back into the chair behind me and motion for her to come sit on my lap. "Face forward," I instruct her when she tries to straddle me. "I don't want to see your face as this dirty pussy rides my cock." Mary lowers herself down onto me, inch after inch, her pussy clenching on the edge of her release. "Do not come until I do," I warn her as I pump up into her. "This cock has been in your filthy ass, and now your eager pussy is sucking it dry. You're a nasty bitch."

"Oh my god, James, yes," she pants as her hips move erratically. "Please cum in my filthy pussy. I need to come so badly."

I don't make her wait much longer. Two thrusts into her and

my head is tipping back as I shout her name, my cum squirting inside of her. She's coming right after, my name slipping from between her lips like a sordid secret.

Mary's head hits my shoulder with a sigh, my cock still buried inside of her, and that's when worry begins to roll over me.

"Was that too much?"

"No." She shakes her head, her words a muffled sound against my shoulder. "It was perfect. Mary ran out of here as soon as you began to fuck my ass."

I laugh against her sweaty neck, inhaling her scent and letting it soothe my trembling insides. "Let's go pack our stuff up. I think we'll be leaving soon."

"I hope Mary doesn't think we should stay after that display." She chuckles as she stands to pull her pants up.

"Let's hope Nick works quickly."

"I can't leave here without Connor. It's not an option," she says adamantly as she tightens the drawstring of her pants. "Not even if he tries to force us to leave. We leave here together or not at all."

"I agree," I reply with a nod and finish zipping my pants up. "Let's go get our stuff together."

Nick

Following Billy and moving quickly, I'm shocked to find him leading me back toward the children's ward.

"The witch is in the children's ward?" I question and Billy wipes at his nose like it's dripping snot again. His form flickers, making the action so contradicting.

"Yeah. She likes to be able to rest her spirit in objects. She also protects the ward as well. She don't let nothin' in here that'll hurt the kids," Billy starts to explain, but I quickly override him.

"How'd Conroy come in then?"

"The moment he stepped into the ward, Shashay was doing

her juju thing. Conroy didn't stay long before he was back as your friend, and then you two got naked," Billy replies, and I flush, not even realizing I jacked me and Connor off in front of a dead child audience. That's some disturbing shit for the record books. Thinking back, Conroy said he was tired and just dropped. That must have been Shashay taking his control away. If that's the case, then we really might have a shot at freeing Connor of Conroy's vile possession of him.

"How will we know which object Shashay is in?" I quickly change the subject, and Billy huffs a laugh at it.

"You got to give an offering. Something that comes from you and only you." Billy passes right through the set of double doors to the ward while I have to struggle to open them again. Doesn't matter, me and Connor came through here recently today. These doors have a force attached to them to purposely keep anything out. Shoving my way in again, Billy has his shoulder propped up on the wall, hands shoved in his pockets, and ankles crossed, waiting.

"What do you mean offer something? Does she want blood? I can prick my finger or something."

Billy laughs and waves for me to follow after him. Each time we pass by a room on our walk, I pause a little, looking into the doorway as activity runs wild. Toys in action with no one playing with them, little ones' laughter bouncing off the walls, even chalk moving and drawing tiny flowers. While the sight chills me to my core, I'm in awe of it all.

"This here's George's room. You ran into him earlier," Billy says, stopping in front of a door that's closed. "He's more than likely got Shashay in there with him. She tends to mother him a lot." He hitches his thumb at the door, and I stare at it.

"Is there some secret knock to get in?" I continue to stare at the door like something is getting ready to jump out and bite me while Billy giggles.

"Just go in," he replies and shoos me to open the door and walk in.

Turning the handle, the creaking of the old, worn-out hinges sends goose bumps along my arms and neck amongst the silence of the halls. Despite all the activity taking place, the only thing to be heard is the echo of wind blowing through the broken windows.

The room is loaded with dolls of all kinds, and I almost turn around and run away. This is some Annie doll shit and I have a moment of why me before putting a pep in my step and continuing forward.

The walls and almost every available surface of the room have dolls that seem to follow each step I take. Even in their worn-out nature, with missing eyeballs, hair, and clothes, they seem to be well-groomed and kept.

"So, which one is she?" I question Billy. When I get no response, I slowly turn around and see he's gone. This little shit has up and left me in a room full of fucking Chucky dolls.

"Billy!" I whisper-shout and get no response. A doll's high-pitched chuckle has me freezing in place. The sound is so sweet and innocent, yet in a place and time like this, nothing but terror can describe it. I get my nerves in check and turn around, seeing one doll on the wall turning its head to face me and blinking one eye since the other looks stuck.

"You were looking for me, yes?" it asks while its creepy little mouth moves along with it.

"Shashay? Yes, I was. Billy thought you could help?" I hold my hands in front of me trying to convey I'm not a threat. It's a mind fuck to be speaking to a child-like doll whose appearance is worn and fragile.

"Ah, Billy. Sweet boy, that one. So, so sad, his past, but heart of gold." The doll's hands move and settle in its lap as that one eye blinks every so often, mimicking a live person. While my soul wants to leave my body, I know damn well I need to go through this.

"Connor…" I start to say, but the doll cuts me off, holding up a hand in front of her to stop my words in their tracks.

"That vile soul possessing your lover's body. Unfortunately, he is far too strong for me to remove him from your friend. The most I can do is put him to sleep for a time. Or send his soul to the beyond."

"That! That second one! I'm pretty sure we won't have a weeping widow mourning him and he won't be able to terrorize the hospital when we leave either. Will it hurt Connor?" I question, biting my lip in thought suddenly unsure about it. My hands tremble slightly with the thought of hurting him after what he's had to endure here.

100

"Your lover will feel some mild discomfort and confusion being separated from Conroy, but he will be back in control of himself." The doll blinks her one eye again as she speaks.

"Okay. What do we need to do? How do we go about this?" I start thinking of all these scenarios as my forehead scrunches and all these satanic rituals start playing out in my mind. If this chick needs an animal sacrifice, I may end up leaving Connor here. I love him, but killing bunnies in the name of spirit banishment is pushing it. My thoughts turn towards the mutt and thinking about her tail wagging happily as if she's just happy to be in our presence. Yeah, Connor's going to have to stay. Jane's the scooby to this mystery gang.

"You will need to lure him back to his cell. The guards that originally trapped him there left runes and a binding spell on his door which kept him contained. The magic is powerful there. You will need to trap him in a salt circle to perform this ritual. Mary stored tons of salt in the kitchen. She found the soup too bland."

I nod and bow like a dumbass, because right now, this little, broken doll feels really powerful and the last thing I want to do is piss her off by insulting her. It's at that moment I remember Billy telling me about giving her something of myself. I reach in my pocket and pull out my knife before slicing through my thumb and leaving a smudge on the floor. A hmm of delight echoes around the room, and Billy reappears almost instantly. I look at his sunken face and another thought hits me.

"Shashay. Is it possible to help souls cross over?" I question as I turn to face the doll again.

"Yes. I assume you'd like to send Billy to rest?" She speaks as her one eye blinks like she's assessing me.

"Only if he'd like that," I reply and turn to face Billy. "You didn't deserve this hell, buddy. You deserve to have peace," I tell him and even though he's a spirit, I swear I almost see tears forming in his eyes.

"I'd like that," he tells me in a small voice that shatters my heart. The horrors this poor little guy has been through were something no kid should ever have to live through.

"Then let's get to work, buddy."

Connor

This psycho is obsessed with children. He's constantly pacing in front of the children's wing, and since he's in my fucking body, it makes me feel filthy. For the past two days, I've felt like a filthy piece of shit.

His eerie chuckle catches me off guard as he runs *my* hand over the door. "It's genetic, ya know, liking little children. I got it from my mama," he tells me, using my voice. "She liked me a whole lot until I grew hair around my cock."

If I was in control of my stomach, I would've fucking puked.

"That witch in there is up to something. I can feel it."

What witch? I think.

"Shashay," he grits out through my teeth. "She's in there with your lover. If you were alive in my day, you'd be in here too for the shit you two pulled earlier. Electroshock would be the only cure. Did you want to try it out? I bet I could get those machines up and running."

No!

"Well damn, I'll let it go since you did seem to like me fucking that little girlfriend of yours. So, not completely gay. You're playing both fields, huh, champ?"

I don't bother to pay attention to him anymore because the man is certifiable. I can't see any way out of this, and he's too strong to overcome. I'll be trapped in here while my friends leave, living their lives without me.

It'd be worth it if I could ensure they were safe.

"Noble," Conroy snickers. "The savior complex, along with being gay, you're special, kid. I think I'll keep you."

A bright light shines through the small window in the door as a jolt of energy brushes past us.

What was that?

"Damn it!" Conroy snarls as he backs away from the door.

"She's sent Billy away."

Away where? Where's Nick?

"To the other side, you dumb shit," he snaps, berating me with my own fucking voice. "Shashay will be coming for us next."

Good.

"Nah, kid. It's not good. It means I have more of a chance leaving this place."

I don't understand what he's talking about, but I do recognize where he's taking us. We head back down the stairs to the basement, the air growing colder as we descend. I wonder where James and Mary are, and if they're okay.

"They're fine," Conroy says with a laugh. "That mountain of a man fucked her asshole in the kitchen. Poor Mary has been hiding ever since. We'll be lucky to find her when we're ready for her to open the doors."

James did what?

Conroy takes us back down the hall of tortures toward his old cell as I begin to imagine James doing that to Mary. *Did she like it?*

"She liked it," Conroy answers. "She liked other things as well, things I could do better for her than all of you."

We're back inside his room, and Jane, the shaggy mutt, raises her tired head with a bark. For some reason, the dog likes Conroy.

"She likes me because I'm an alpha. It's in the energy." He taps my chest. "The rest of you are a bunch of pussies."

Why are we in this room?

"Because they will come here to set you free. This room is filled with magic, couldn't you feel it when you first broke in?"

Now that he mentions it, I do remember. The way it was clean and smelled fresh. Even with his bones laying inside the straitjacket, it didn't smell like a body had been decaying in here for decades.

"Because I was sealed in here, never to leave, and nothing to penetrate. A spell given to them by the witch upstairs."

Nick will never agree to letting you leave with us.

"He won't have a choice, and he won't say anything because he's in love with you."

I know Conroy is right. Nick would deceive his brother and Mary if it meant I got out of here. He has some hero complex, and I know he'll be thinking he can take care of Conroy later, as long as he gets me out first.

"That's right," Conroy hums as he stretches out on his small cot, my feet hanging over the edge. "I'll finally be free of this place, and then the real fun will begin."

We should've never come here. We should've gone to Silent Night Theme Park instead. As soon as James heard of an insane asylum, that was it. There was no other option. I bet Silent Night is a walk in the fucking park. After this, I don't care how rich we are. No more Phantom Chasers.

"Your boyfriend upstairs will disagree. He's had a taste for sending the dead to the other side. He's going to want to save all the souls he can now."

He's right again. Nick is like an open book. He's sarcastic, loud-mouthed, and crass, but he wears his heart on his sleeve and he's a softy for children. Probably because the four of us suffered when we were kids.

"Not one of you knew true suffering," Conroy spits out. "So what if your parents were drunks and forgot to feed you? So what if James and Nick had broom handles broken over their backs, or even that sweet little girl getting fucked by her uncle? None of it compares to actual torture."

Why do you want to continue dealing with torture when you know what it's like to receive it?

"Look how I turned out. Strong, invincible, and I can take anything standing. The world needs tougher people."

I like the world the way it is.

"You need to be tougher too." He sits up and looks expectantly at the door. "Don't worry, I'll help you."

I don't want you to make me tough.

104

"Do you hear that?" he asks, our heart rate climbing with excitement. "Oh! It sounds like they found the salt!"

What salt?

"Thanks for talking to me," he murmurs as I hear Nick's voice grow louder in the corridor. "I think I can convince them I'm you now."

NO!

"Conroy!" Nick calls out just as he steps over the threshold. He looks so good with his messed-up hair and excited eyes. "We're here to get rid of you for good."

"You think so?" Conroy says as he continues to stretch out on the bed. "Are you making something with that salt?"

James and Mary walk in next, and I can just feel the sexual energy pouring off of them.

"Your friend is jealous you fucked Mary in the ass," Conroy reveals.

Fuck! Take it back!

"You fucked Mary in the ass?" Nick turns to look at James, always so fucking easily distracted.

"Can we talk about this later?" James groans as he grabs the bag of salt he took from the kitchen.

"We will be talking about this later for sure," Nick mumbles as Mary's cheeks redden. I hate that they're embarrassing her.

"Connor doesn't like the way you're making the little one jealous," Conroy tells them.

"He'll be fine when we discuss with Mary which hole she'd rather us in. If James worked out the tight one, any of us can get in," Nick says as he begins to haul Conroy and the bed away from the wall.

"Nick!" Mary exclaims, her cheeks growing redder, only this time, I see lust swirling in her eyes too.

"Oh, I can't wait to fuck her little ass," Conroy coos, and I'm once again reminded of the severity of our situation. I can't let us both leave.

James begins to form a large salt circle around the bed as Conroy sits up, resting his elbows on his crossed legs and watching closely.

"Why aren't you fighting us?" James demands as he drops the empty salt bag.

"Because that's sugar," Conroy states. Nick bends forward to grab some, dipping his tongue into his palm. He begins to sputter and spit as Conroy falls back on the bed laughing. "You're dumb as shit."

"Ignore him." James presses a hand to Nick's chest, effectively stopping him from tackling Conroy. "Let's get this done so we can leave."

"Connor," Nick says as he stares into my eyes. "We're going to weaken this piece of shit, and when we do, we need you to shove him out."

"This is exciting." Conroy rubs my hands together, a smile on my face. "What do we do first?"

I ignore the ritual they're doing. The candles and the chanting aren't going to do a fucking thing to dispel this monster, and I can't face the fact that I'll be trapped here without them.

I don't want to be without my family.

"Guys?" Conroy says in the perfect imitation of me. He rubs at his eyes and squints, pretending to be blind.

"Connor!" Nick stands, sweat pouring down from his temples. "Push him out."

"I don't think I can," Conroy continues, sniffing for further effect.

Is this how I sound? Weak and scared?

"You can, Connor!" James exclaims. "I believe in you."

He thinks I'm weak too, and the way Mary is looking at me, tells me she's not so sure I can do it either.

Conroy grunts and squeezes my eyes shut, sealing my friends off of my sight and sounding like he's taking the biggest shit of his life. A small snort escapes him at my thoughts, and I feel myself becoming more depressed. I really don't want to be trapped with him forever, alone, inside these walls.

They continue to chant, and that's when I feel it, a warmth gathering in the pit of my stomach. It grows hotter as it spreads out, and when it feels near the point of unbearable pain, my vision blurs. I am once again in control of my body, and even though he's barely detectable, Conroy is still inside of me.

"Connor?" Mary's shaking voice interrupts my thoughts, and I squint to look at her.

"I'm so sorry, Mary," I choke out and she runs for me, wrapping her arms around my waist.

"Out of the circle!" Nick hisses, yanking us over the thick salt line. "He won't be able to escape that."

He can and he has.

Mary has her arms still wrapped firmly around my waist when Nick leans in, grabbing my face between his hands and kissing me. It's the first time we've done anything in front of Mary and his brother, and I can't help but feel hopeful.

We will be able to get rid of Conroy. I'll tell Nick as soon as we're home.

"Let's get upstairs, guys," James says. "I don't want to stay a minute longer."

Nick grabs me around the waist, supporting me as we rush upstairs. I hope with everything inside me, the headless Mary lets us go. I can't stay here.

"She's there." Mary points to the top of the stairs. I don't see anything. "Mary, can we go?"

There are a few moments of silence, the kind that twists my stomach into knots until I see the tension bleed from our Mary's shoulders.

"She says we can leave, but we have to make it quick."

James hurries off to grab our cots and equipment, and Mary chases after him to help. Nick leads me to the doors and grabs the handle. He takes a deep breath and pulls, laughing when it opens easily.

"We're free, Connor!" he exclaims.

I want to feel the excitement with him, but all I feel is fear. What am I doing? What if I'm never free of this monster inside of me?

Nick deposits me in the van and pulls my glasses out of his pocket. I slip them on and groan when one lens is cracked.

"We'll get you new ones," he says. "I gotta go help them get the rest of the stuff. You'll be okay?"

I nod as he leans forward, pressing his lips to my forehead. Then he runs into the house as my heart lurches up in my throat at the sight. What if headless Mary decides to close the doors again?

I don't exhale the breath I'm holding until James hops in the driver's seat while Mary slides into the back with me, slipping her hand into mine. Nick ushers Jane the dog into the back, and then climbs into the passenger seat. I hope this means she forgives me for what I did to her, for what *he* did to her.

We're going to have so much fun, pet.

Bedlam's Playground

EPILOGUE

It's nice being back on the outside. To breathe in the fresh air and feel the sunshine on my face… Even if it is only for short periods of time. I don't know what spell that witch gave to these children, but I truly am locked inside this kid's body for most of the day.

But I can grow stronger, and I would take anything over being in that looney bin.

"People are suggesting Silent Night Theme Park," James says, looking at us excitedly. "You guys wanted to do that one before Belgrove was suggested."

"I don't want to go to another haunted place," Mary whines, causing Jane to bark from her spot at my feet.

"It did make us so much money though." Nick leans forward to haul her into his lap. "We could buy a house soon and move out of this crummy apartment."

"What do you think, Connor?" James asks the twerp. "You haven't said much."

Fuck, time to sound like a fucking pussy.

"I don't know." I sniff and shove up these geeky glasses. "If Mary is all right with it, then I guess I can do it."

If I can leave this apartment for longer than a few hours a day, I would go fucking anywhere. Except Belgrove.

But a theme park would have children, right?

I always did love my little girls.

AUTHOR NOTE

Guys! I wrote a book with CA FREAKING RENE! Listen, I may be an author but I'm still allowed to fangirl ok? I hope that this little bit of what me and Chrissy have to offer you keeps you on edge and ready for more, because the plans we have blow even my mind!

As always, Thank you to my girls and thank you to my readers for being the absolute best people I've ever had the pleasure of meeting, even if it's just through my work. You all keep me fueled and ready to give you more.

Chrissy, you have been a balm on my wounded soul and I cannot thank you enough for your love and support.

Stay tuned, there's more boo's around the bin. ;)

Follow me everywhere if you dare:

https://linktr.ee/StoryBrooksAuthor

ALSO BY STORY BROOKS

The Deadly Seven Series

(Co-Write with Cassie Hargrove)

(Dark Contemporary)

1. Obsession

2. Seduction

3. Devotion

4. Salvation

The Phantom Chasers Series (Co-Write with CA Rene)

(Dark Contemporary)

1. Bedlams Playground

2. Silent Night Theme Park

Unnecessary Intentions(Contemporary)

1. Disrespected

Game Of Survival Series (Paranormal Fantasy)

1. The Reaping

2. The Chase

1. Foreverland (Peter Pan Retelling)

ABOUT THE AUTHOR

Story Brooks, also known as Cat Vann, lives in South Carolina with her husband, three kids, and plenty of animals running about.

Story has always been a reader first and dedicated book worm. She loves connecting with other readers and authors in the book world and discovering new inspiration to fuel her passion of writing.

ACKNOWLEDGMENTS

Writing with Story AKA my Kitty Cat has been so much fun! These stories have our signature humor but also deal with real life issues. I had a feeling we would mesh well and I'm so glad she let me tackle her into this series! Love you, Cat!

To all our Betas and readers! You guys make being an author worth every drop of blood, sweat and tears. Thank you for reading our stories.

ALSO BY C.A. RENE

Check out www.careneauthor.com/links for all my backlist!

ABOUT C.A. RENE

The computer screen is my canvas and the keyboard is my brush. Thank you for viewing my masterpieces. My addictions include coffee, books, and WINE, in that order.

Please join my FB Group and show the love! I appreciate it!

C.A.'S Renegades

www.ingramcontent.com/pod-product-compliance
Lightning Source LLC
Chambersburg PA
CBHW061254170626
46809CB00007B/2989